About the Author

Göksel Altınışık was born in 1969 in Ankara, Turkey. She works as a pulmonologist at Pamukkale University. She also has a master's degree in sociology. She previously published a poetry book and four storybooks in Turkish, published by Lakin Yayınları. She co-authored a poetry book and a storybook with her spouse, Ali Ergur, published by Mantis Yayınları. Her latest work, titled *COVID Patients Behind the Glass Wall*, based on her sociology master's thesis, has been published by Raskolnikov Kitap. Göksel Altınışık continues to work as a writer, a physician, and a sociologist, and is listed in the New Turkish Literature Dictionary.

Self-Written Stories

Göksel Altınışık

Self-Written Stories

Olympia Publishers
London

www.olympiapublishers.com
OLYMPIA PAPERBACK EDITION

Copyright © Göksel Altınışık 2024

The right of Göksel Altınışık to be identified as author of
this work has been asserted in accordance with sections 77 and 78 of
the Copyright, Designs and Patents Act 1988.

All Rights Reserved

No reproduction, copy or transmission of this publication
may be made without written permission.
No paragraph of this publication may be reproduced,
copied or transmitted save with the written permission of the publisher,
or in accordance with the provisions
of the Copyright Act 1956 (as amended).

Any person who commits any unauthorized act in relation to
this publication may be liable to criminal
prosecution and civil claims for damage.

A CIP catalog record for this title is
available from the British Library.

ISBN: 978-1-83543-045-3

This is a work of fiction.
Names, characters, places and incidents originate from the writer's
imagination. Any resemblance to actual persons, living or dead, is
purely coincidental.

First Published in 2024

Olympia Publishers
Tallis House
2 Tallis Street
London
EC4Y 0AB

Printed in Great Britain

Dedication

To Özge and Ali, who hear me even from the things I haven't told.

Acknowledgments

I extend my gratitude to my immediate family and close friends for encouraging me to write this book, as well as to the anonymous protagonists who entrusted me with their untold stories, generously sharing their hope for healing, both for themselves and for others.

Everybody Hurts

"I heard that he died... in a car accident." Her voice was normal until this point. Then, she added, "He was trapped in the car..."

The tone in her voice sent shivers down my spine. There was also the influence of another imaginary scene that came to my mind. There was a long silence between us, enough time for me to gather myself.

How did this story begin and where did it go? At some point, I even said, "She must have had so much to tell!" But I could never have predicted such an ending.

After reading my first storybook, she found my work phone number through a friend of mine. When she called, she mentioned his name. She said she would come by to have her book signed. A week passed, and she called again, informing me that she would visit the next day. It happened to be a moment when I had no work to attend to. In fact, just as I heard her voice say "Hello" at my door, I was thinking of taking a break and doing something for myself. Her voice had a soothing quality, like the sound of flowing water. I had heard it while I was busy signing a few documents. I raised my head and looked toward the door. When I saw her, my feeling was confirmed. There was a calmness in her glide into my room, her gentle seating in the guest chair, and the way she extended my book to me with her slender fingers, resting it on the table.

I took the book. As always, a smile spread across my face when I saw its cover. I had believed in that project so much. I was happy not only for its success but also for it becoming tangible and shareable. It was a collection of letters that I had carried within me for a long time and finally poured onto paper. In my opinion, the greatest joy for a collector is the feeling they experience when they exhibit their amassed objects years later. That smile was a reflection of that sentiment.

I needed to ask for her name to sign the book. It would be an acquaintance. On the day of a usual book signing, sitting in front of a table adorned with a white tablecloth and a vase filled with daisies, on a wooden chair, if a reader was waiting in the queue before me, I would ask, "Whom shall I sign it for?" and do the necessary. Her visit to my room indicated that she wouldn't just take the book and leave; on the contrary, she would stay a while, and we would have a conversation. I didn't mind it actually, as I had enough time. Besides, she had reached out to me through a close friend. I asked for her name.

"Derin," she said.

Just as I was about to sign, I paused. "There's a lovely café nearby. They make delicious carrot and walnut cakes. I've been craving it since morning. Shall we go there?" I suggested.

She clapped her hands with childlike joy; it meant she said yes. But I didn't fully understand the sentence she added afterward at that moment, "Besides, you should also listen to my story."

I put the book in my bag. I was glad that I would have time to think about what to write as autograph. I had to search for the keys for a while. I found them in the pocket of my jacket, hanging on the back of the chair. The weather could be cool. So, I took my jacket with me. While I was dealing with these things, she had gotten up and headed toward the door. I followed her. She was very thin, but she stood firmly on the ground. She didn't seem like she would sway or falter. Her blonde hair was long, reaching her waist. She had tied a tuft of it at the back with a white ribbon. I tried to guess her age. In this state, she looked like a high school student, but my friend had told me that she worked as an advertising executive in a big agency. So, she must be one of those ageless women.

We were going somewhere nearby. It seemed like rain was about to fall. I wanted to get my car to avoid getting caught in a downpour on the way back. She walked with me all the way to the parking lot. When I headed toward the car, it was bizarre that she said, "I know where we're going, and it's very close. I can walk there." I didn't have a chance to object. She had already set off. It was drizzling lightly. Actually, I thought about how much I used to enjoy walking in this kind of weather. I raised the collar of my jacket and hurried to catch up with her. She turned her head slightly, looked at me, and smiled. We walked together.

Compared to my previous visits, the café had fewer customers. Perhaps it was because we had come at a time outside of meal hours. However, I was going to show off my choice of dining, indicating that many people preferred this place. As I headed toward the busier corner, I noticed that she gestured in the opposite direction.

"I don't want what I'm going to tell you to be overheard. Can we sit at that table by the window?" she said.

We sat at one of the tables known as the gossip table, with chairs placed close to each other. It was warm inside. I took off my jacket and casually draped it over the armrest. On the other hand, she had lost her initial relaxed attitude. She closed the front of her wool jacket and crossed her arms over her belly. I couldn't figure out the meaning behind this gesture of closing herself off.

I listened to the music. It was a familiar melody. I tried to figure out which song it was. It was an R.E.M. song "Everybody hurts." I had started singing the song to myself when she lifted her head and locked eyes with mine. She seemed about to say something but then leaned back again upon seeing the waiter approaching to take our order. I asked her what she wanted. She made a gesture as if it didn't matter. It was the carrot and walnut cake that had brought us there. I ordered two cakes and two teas, and added that one of the teas should be a bright red one. She didn't make a sound. The waiter left. Derin was still silent. I thought she postponed speaking because she didn't want to interrupt the conversation further. I waited. I went back to singing the song in my mind. And at that moment, it ended anyway; "Everybody hurts. You're not alone."

In a short time, the waiter brought us what we ordered.

"Bright red tea?" he asked.

The silence had settled so deeply between us that I couldn't speak. I tapped the table in front of me twice with the four fingers of my right hand. The waiter placed my tea right there. He scattered the others on the table in a way he deemed suitable. He left our order slip on the table and walked away. I took a sip of my tea, almost slurping it. I was now reacting against the silence. I took a big bite of my cake. When I made the sound of my sip, she raised her head once again. She watched me as I bit into the cake. Then suddenly, she started speaking. "Some of your stories have deeply affected me. In some, I found traces of my own experiences. In others, I could put myself in the place of the story's protagonist," she said. *Ah,* I thought, *let her start praising my writing, of course.* After all, we were there as a writer and a reader, or so I thought. She continued, "I believe that writing holds immense power. With your words, you can impact the lives of people you don't know, and whom you will never know. You can make them feel they are not alone. You can persuade them to do or not to do something." I was preparing to object. Not any writer wrote with such thoughts. Such a sense of responsibility would be the biggest obstacle to creativity. Before I could say these things, she added, "You can even save lives." No way! I looked at her, and she was dead serious.

After that, it was almost like a monologue. She spoke, and I listened. I responded with my expressions, changing glances, and occasional sounds of approval or surprise. Occasionally, I interjected a few sentences, but they didn't carry much meaning. Mostly, I listened. Initially, it felt like a duty, but as time went on, my interest grew, and my emotions kept changing…

I want to tell you my story. Please allow me to tell it until the end. I will start from years ago, but I don't want to bore you with excessive details. I only want you to understand the events and interpret the circumstances that led me to that point. I'm sharing most of them for the first time.

It was many years ago. I had just finished high school, but I couldn't pass the university entrance exam that year. I was studying at home and working at a dry-cleaning shop owned by a friend of my father. It was within walking distance from our street. I would go to work early in the morning and return home before it got dark in the evening. During this time, someone had started following my comings and goings. I didn't notice. One day, he appeared in front of me, blocking my path, and I was terrified. Even though I thought to myself, "What harm can he do in broad daylight, in the middle of the road?" I was scared. He explained that he lived in the two adjacent buildings. He had been following me for a while. He liked me a lot and couldn't get me out of his mind. When he told he wanted to meet me and see each other, I suddenly panicked. "That's impossible," I said. I quickly slipped past him and rushed into the shop. My coworkers gathered around, worried about my breathless state. The large machine had just started running, filling the room with intense hot steam. It helped me catch my breath. I reassured those around me, saying, "There's no problem."

I was walking restlessly on that short road. It felt like he would appear in front of me again at any moment. I wasn't scared, but sometimes it felt like I could see him in the distant corners. It seemed that his face had imprinted itself in my memory during our encounter. I didn't mention this incident to anyone at home. My father might not allow me to work, and my mother wouldn't have a say in such a situation. I was allowed to work because I promised that I would pass the exam. That's why I would study constantly at night after finishing household chores. Thoughts like having a boyfriend or going out for fun didn't cross my mind. First, I needed self-reliance. For that, I had to study and become a professional. Economic independence was important for my freedom. Although I knew my parents loved me very much, I had a family that restricted my life. I had no intention of going from my father's house to a husband's house. But it seemed that he had no intention of giving up either. In fact, he seemed even more determined when I rejected his proposal. He phoned the dry-cleaning shop several times, asking to speak to me. Of course, the shop owner, who was my father's friend, didn't agree with such a thing. When the calls persisted, my boss questioned me. After learning that it was an insistence against my will, he put an end to it by saying, "Don't call this place again."

A few days later, a woman came to the shop. We thought she was a customer. Usually, I wouldn't be the one to greet the customers, but at that moment, I was the only one without any work. She came directly to me. She said she came to speak about her son. She told me that I should know what a good opportunity I had missed. I couldn't grasp what she meant at first, as I was preparing to discuss an order with a customer. Then I understood who she was talking about. She described her son. His name was Murat, and he was five years older than me. He had graduated from university and worked at his father's factory. I had captured his attention, and he definitely wanted to talk. His intention was not a one-day wonder. Moreover, we were children from the same neighborhood. Among all the things she said, her last words created a warmth within me. I don't know if it was because of the old Turkish movies or TV series I watched. Our story turned into a romantic tale. Yet, there were no more old films or old neighborhoods left... Determined to keep them alive, I spoke in a dialog-like manner, "Then, let him come and seek my father's approval."

They sent a message; they were demanding a formal visit. The old movie was going on. Since my father knew about my previous opposition to such matters, he sent my mother to persuade me. "She'll definitely refuse, but ask her anyway," he said.

"Let them come and talk," I replied. This time, my father bypassed my mother and came directly to talk to me.

"You were going to study, and no one could have changed your mind on this path," he said. He was right. I told him that I hadn't changed my decision. I added that if this were to happen, I would present one condition; I wouldn't be prevented from attending university! After we got to know each other, a final decision would be made. By then, I would have taken the exam. We could prolong the engagement, and I might even reach my final year. I couldn't determine the emotion that drove me to make these plans. Perhaps my heart had taken a turn. I was young; I wanted to love and be loved. I wanted to experience the feeling of love that my friends described with butterflies on their tongues. Moreover, he was handsome. He was taller than me, which was important to me due to my above-average height. And his voice trembled when he spoke to me. I took it as a sign of the value he placed on me.

They came. Flowers, chocolates... Heart-shaped chocolates arranged in a silver gondola, adorned with white tulle and pink ribbons. It was the most romantic package I had ever seen. Tulle and pink ribbons... I wondered if he had asked someone about it. He had brought a large bouquet of red roses. Each one was a bud, and a small card was attached. I had never heard of putting a note in a proposal flower. This one was already hidden among the leaves. My heart raced as I took the note and concealed it in the palm of my hand. I was going crazy to know what it said. I could only think of the bathroom. Leaving the guests in the living room, I placed the bouquet and chocolates on the table and went to the corridor. I went to the bathroom. I opened the note. I felt like I was going to faint. It was written in neat handwriting, *You can give me the world...* Due to the intense emotions, I was experiencing at that moment, this note felt like the most beautiful promise in the world. After wiping away my tears and fixing my makeup, I looked at myself in the mirror one last time and said, *"You've got it!"*

I interrupted. "You've given up on your dreams of going to university very quickly. Weren't you going to stand on your own legs? You've easily succumbed to the idea of leaving your father's house and entering the husband's house, pouring cold water on your dreams," I said.

She seemed a bit taken aback by the interruption, fidgeting in her seat. It was as if I hadn't spoken at all, as she continued her narrative.

The rest was like a dream world. I was experiencing love for the first time. And fully... I had only managed to bring up the topic of going to university once. When I said I wanted to get education to become a teacher in the elementary school, he replied, "You will be the head teacher of our children at home." I found it so touching. I was much happier discussing our future together.

There were a few places we frequented. After we had exchanged engagement rings, we could meet freely. He would pick me up from home in his yellow Volkswagen Beetle. We would go to a tea garden with wildflowers in vases on the tables, listening to the song "You're like a daisy, white and delicate..." from the cassette. I saw the alignment of our tastes as a miracle. On such a day, he took my hands in his, gently pressed my palms against his face, and placed kisses on them. He looked into my eyes and said, "I don't want to wait any longer for you to become my wife. I can't bear to be separated from you even for a moment. Let's go and set a wedding date."

We scheduled a date for three months later and arranged to meet in the evening to tell both of our families at the same time. That night, for the first time, I was afraid of my future 'mother-in-law.' When we broke the news, her face turned so dark that if I didn't know better, I could have thought she didn't want me. "I wish you had consulted the elders first," she said. I couldn't understand what there was to consult when everyone was already in agreement about our marriage. Without saying a word, I looked at Murat. He had lowered his head. I did the same.

We rented an apartment in their building. I was about to object. He caressed my hair and said, "Usually, your parents are in the village. Isn't it good for us to be close to my mother for taking care of our baby?" Once again, he had deflated my sails. I don't know what it was about this baby issue; it softened me perfectly.

Our household items were being purchased. Each time, Murat's mother accompanied us. She always somehow opposed my requests for more comfortable, light-colored, and simple furniture; "A white couch? It gets dirty too quickly, and wiping it makes the color fade." "You can't have a display cabinet; where will all the glasses, cups, and crystal be showcased?" "Is there only going to be a brass plank-bed and a mirror wardrobe in the bedroom? I guess you're kidding." Every time she objected, I looked at Murat's face. He always lowered his head. If I had something to say, he silenced me and quietly spoke about the validity of his mother's words. I was feeling uneasy inside, but it was impossible for me to show it. I couldn't even open up about the matter to my own parents. If they said, "You wanted this," I had nothing to say in return.

I had my eye on a curtain for my dream kitchen, where I imagined cooking delicious meals. Every time I passed by the curtain shop, I would stop and gaze at it through the display window. It was a blue roller blind, the color of the sky, with faint, blurry clouds. Even when I closed the blind, I would still be able to gaze at the sky through my window. When it came time to choose a kitchen curtain, the three of us went again. I showed the one I had chosen, but my mother-in-law wanted a different one... No, I said, I want this one. "Did your mother's house have a roller blind too?" she asked.

I was shocked by what was happening. This time, I didn't look at Murat. If I couldn't find his eyes, I would feel very lonely. "We don't have to decide right now. Let's look at other stores," I said. I was trying to buy some time in my own way.

Somehow, Murat and I had chosen the wedding invitation cards together and placed the order. The only thing left was to pick them up by paying the remaining balance. The print shop was conveniently located on our way. I needed a small victory desperately. I had described and had the invitations made exactly as I had always dreamed of. They were adorned with pink tulle and ribbons and placed in heart-shaped envelopes. Murat loved them too. My mother-in-law took one of the invitations in her hand and exclaimed, "What is this, for God's sake? Childish... How can I give this to my acquaintances? Will you embarrass me?" Despite my previous experiences, I had hope in Murat this time. I turned to look at him. Our eyes met this time. I looked at him as if saying, "Please be on my side." At that moment, I saw it and understood. It wasn't going to happen.

Moreover, he spoke in a way that left no room for doubt: "If it doesn't work, let's choose another one now." In that instant, a strange feeling passed through me: absence. I wasn't there in the eyes of the man I claimed to love...

I took off my engagement ring without even realizing it and placed it in Murat's palm. "It's over," I said, "there's no need to continue this any longer." I continued, "I have been marrying your mother all this time without even realizing it. I don't want to."

I was walking away when he started shouting, "Stop! Where are you going? It's not over until I say it's over. Stop, I'm telling you. If you walk out that door, you can never come back to me."

I stopped, turned slowly, looked directly into his eyes, and said, "I'm leaving for good."

At this point, I interrupted once again. Since I started listening to her, it was the first time I truly felt the need to speak. I told her how important it was for her to be able to do this at such a young age and during a time when emotions like love and passion are at their strongest.

"There are always signs of what's coming, but we choose to ignore them. You have been able to see them, despite being in love," I said. I had started to think that she was a very strong woman.

"I haven't finished telling you everything. If you don't mind, don't make a hasty judgment," she said. She had managed to pique my curiosity. I immediately fell silent, and she continued her story.

I arrived home and called my mother and father into the living room. The radio was playing loudly, as usual. "How did it happen? I fell in love with you; oh, I wish I hadn't..." The sound of the radio abruptly cutting off was heard. I had them sit side by side on the couch while I took a seat across from them. "I just returned the engagement ring to Murat. I told him I won't marry him. Please understand me," I said.

I explained what had happened. They looked at each other, and without saying a word, as if they understood each other, my father started, "Do you have something to be ashamed of, my daughter?" I understood what he meant.

I quickly responded, knowing that this was the most important issue for them. "No, Dad, there's nothing I should be ashamed of!" I could feel their sudden relief. It was the first time my father had made a comment since our engagement.

"He always had an attitude of belittling others. We said yes because you wanted it, my daughter. Don't be upset; we are always on your side. You are precious to us more than the rest of the world. It will be as you want it to be." And from then on, they kept their word.

He was holding my hand; we were hugging. We used to go to the cinema. We would sit in the back row. We usually choose films with fewer viewers. He was the first man I kissed. I was in love, and this feeling was boiling in my blood. However, I had implied that we shouldn't go any further before we got married; saying, *"Let's not rush things, OK?"* He kissed my forehead and said he would wait. He really didn't push; in fact, he respected my wish, which made me feel more respected. When the breakup happened, as soon as I got over the initial shock, this came to my mind, and I said, *"Thank goodness..."* Otherwise, I wouldn't have been able to look my father in the face and say, *"I have nothing to be ashamed of,"* with pride.

If we hadn't separated, our wedding would have been a week later. When invitees heard that the engagement was broken, they were very surprised. No one understood the reason, and they couldn't ask us for details. I could guess that various gossips were being spread behind us, but suddenly, a sense of carelessness engulfed me, and I didn't even think about this possibility. A few days later, Murat's mother called my mother. *"What have you raised? As if your daughter is the only fish in the see... Tensions before the wedding always happen, but throwing away the ring because I didn't like the invitation cards. It's something your childish daughter would do. And what you don't understand is that we have a really good reputation. What you did is unacceptable. Let's reconcile and not make a spectacle of ourselves,"* she said.

Of course, she knocked down a notch. It was the first time my mother said, "What kind of people are these?" about anybody.

When it became clear that they wouldn't leave us alone, we went to the village. My father left my mother and me there and went back. We couldn't live in this neighborhood any more. We sold our house for a bargain prize but asked the buyer for some time. We thought we would return once things calmed down to move permanently. I turned off my phone. I didn't want to talk to anyone. I absolutely refused to receive any news. A month and a half passed like this. I hoped that things had calmed down by now. I wanted to continue my life where I had left off and start building a new future for myself. What surprised me the most was how resolute and strong I felt. We were packing our belongings to move. That's when I realized it. I had taken all my photos and personal belongings, even my diaries, to the house where I had dreamed of spending a lifetime. Clothes and other things could be bought again, but I couldn't leave my memories, my past, and my most precious things behind. I sent a message to Murat through a mutual friend. I asked Murat to send my mentioned belongings with him. I was devastated when I found out that he refused. Our friend carried his response, "Don't we have any decency left? Let her come and get the belongings from me," which made me feel ashamed of what I had done. Furthermore, he added saying, "Can't we say goodbye to each other and wish each other happiness like two modern people?" I reluctantly accepted his suggestion. I was determined and strong enough to resist if he insisted on reuniting, anyway. I called him from a payphone and asked when I could collect my belongings. He informed me of the time he would be waiting for me in front of an ice cream shop we had visited a few times before. I went there, but he hadn't arrived yet.

A little later, I saw Murat in a different car. He stopped in front of me. I thought to myself, so he changed his car. It was for the best. It would have been very difficult for me to get back in the yellow Volkswagen, where I had experienced the happiest moments of my life. I waited for him to get out of the car. He opened the automatic window on my side and said, "Come on, get in. Let's sit somewhere and talk. Then I'll give you your belongings." I hesitated, but it had come this far; I didn't want to leave without taking what was mine. At the same time, I thought to myself, Let's not go to the village cafe, at least. After all, we both would be saddened by the beautiful memories there.

I got in the car. It started moving toward the main road. I asked where we were going. He said that a new place had opened at the end of the street. I was uneasy, but how could the person I trusted all this time do something bad to me? I just wanted to get away from him as soon as possible and never see his face again. While I was thinking about how he had killed the feelings inside me, my uneasiness increased when we passed the place he mentioned. At that very moment, the car doors locked automatically from his side. He continued to drive the car fast without answering any of my questions. He turned onto a forest road. I was desperately trying to force the door open. If it opened, I would jump out of the car without thinking.

We stopped on the side of the road in the forest. He turned to me and calmly said, "I told you we would talk. What's the rush?" I pleaded with him to take me back, told him that what he was doing was wrong and that he couldn't force me to come here. He told me how much he missed me, couldn't forget about me, and wanted to start again. It's over, I said, we can't be together any more. "I told you, it won't be over until I say it's over," he *shouted. His eyes were looking distant. It was as if he couldn't see me. I started hitting him. He grabbed my wrists with one hand. Meanwhile, the seat reclined backward. Before I reacted, he was on top of me. I tried pushing him off, but it was impossible. I was trapped. I was crying, screaming, begging. None of it was working. He didn't stop. As the pain intensified, I screamed as if my throat was being torn apart. He pressed his body against mine. I could hear his breath mixed with a growl in my ear.*

At that moment, she fell silent. I was frozen in shock. Even if she spoke, I couldn't listen to the rest at that moment. I couldn't find any words to say. I looked around. From the outside, we must have looked a certain way because the waiter didn't approach us. The surrounding tables were empty. I had no sense of time. I didn't know how long we had been there or what time it was. What I had heard had shattered me, but I had started to become curious about the rest. What would I do if she stopped telling the story? She might not continue. I couldn't comprehend how she managed to recount even this much. When we first came to the cafe, I thought we wouldn't stay long. When I caught a whiff of the delicious coffee aroma, I briefly thought to myself, *Shall we have a cup of coffee?* At the point where the conversation had reached, I wasn't in a state to enjoy a strong Turkish coffee or anything else.

I thought about what had happened. I had come to the cafe to have my book signed and ended up sitting with a young woman I had never met before. While expecting compliments, I learned about her life story, even the most intimate moments. From dreams of a young girl, wedding preparations, a strong decision made without worrying about what others would say, to rebuilding a life... It was like a stabbing scene from a tabloid news article. In this brief but intense time I knew her, I felt that she could overcome any problem. What intrigued me was how she managed to stand on her own legs, evident in every aspect of the person sitting across from me.

She had been betrayed by someone she trusted, someone she never even considered would harm her. She had been hurt by the one closest to her. Had she chosen to act as if it had never happened? Had she been able to find her way again after long psychiatric support sessions? Had she been courageous enough to go to court and ensure she faced the consequences by revealing what had happened? Did her family know? If they found out, how would they react to this situation that I presumed would devastate them? I waited with various questions in my mind. Her lips parted. She began to speak without looking at me.

After a while, when he started to breathe more calmly, he straightened up. "I should have done this to you much earlier. This is what you deserve!" he said. The pain he had caused me and the sense of emptiness aside, those words themselves were the ultimate destruction. "This is what you deserve... This is what you deserve..." If I didn't do what he wanted, this is what I would deserve... These words echoed in my mind, and most of all, I realized how the feeling I had mistaken for love had been tainted.

Such a great hatred filled me that, taking advantage of the power his betrayal had given me and his relaxed state, I managed to push his body to the side. I straightened up and started punching the window. The glass shattered. I still don't know how I managed to do that. Moreover, I even managed to throw myself out of that window. I started running away. Wherever I could escape to... He got out of the car crazily. He ran after me. He easily caught me. He leaned me against the nearest tree, facing away from me, lifted my skirt, and... In pain, I dug my nails into the tree. Then, as he dragged me back into the car, I looked at the cuts on my arms, the fresh blood seeping from my bleeding nails, and the splinters of wood under my nails. I felt empty inside; my soul had left me. He sat me back in the seat. My mind was filled with the warmth flowing from between my legs and the life seeping through my palms. I no longer felt what was happening around me. We had started driving and arrived in front of the house. We stopped suddenly with a screech. I sat motionless, like a corpse. He reached over and opened the door, saying, "Now go. But don't forget, you can still give me the world. I want you back." My clothes were torn. I tried to gather myself and quickly entered the apartment, taking advantage of the darkness falling.

I don't remember how I opened the door or how I got in the shower. I regained some composure with the effect of the cold water. I wished the water flowing down my head would take me along with it through the drain. When I grew tired from trembling, I turned off the water and stepped out of the bathroom. At that moment, I remembered the note he had placed among the red roses. It was focused on taking away all expectations from me. He had gotten what he wanted. I felt so worthless that I didn't have the right to live. I knew I couldn't look into my parents' eyes. I had shattered their world, too. Thankfully, they weren't home and hadn't seen me in that predicament.

As if lost in the land of dreams, with unsteady steps, I went to the kitchen. I took the rat poison from under the sink, from some hidden place. It was a small bottle. I opened the cap and brought the bottle to my mouth. When I tilted my head back, the poison flowed down my throat warmly. I went to my room. I lay down on my bed. For one last sleep. To never wake up again...

I couldn't believe that she had chosen to die. To end her pain, she intended to destroy her own body, which she believed had become worthless. I was very relieved that she had failed. It felt as if I had found Derin in that sleep. She wanted to be irreversible, as if I was trying to wake her up. Suddenly, I put myself in her shoes. I could understand her vulnerability at that age, her vulnerability, disappointment, and most of all, the guilt that comes with being deceived. She had mentioned that she had gone into a sleep from which she never intended to wake up. She continued to narrate from there.

I woke up. I could barely open my eyes. When I tried to sit up, I felt a sharp pain in my throat. I was tied to the bed, and the tube they had inserted into my stomach had become taut as I tried to sit up. I never forgot that pain. And the peace I felt when I said, "I'm alive." I calmly lay back on the bed. I tightly closed my eyes and screamed internally multiple times, "I'm alive! I'm alive! I'm alive!" It was as if I spoke to myself outside of my body, saying, "Live from now on, Derin. You must live."

After a while, I learned how I ended up there. My cousin was supposed to stay with me that night. She had the keys. When she came home, she found me unconscious in bed, called an ambulance, dressed me in clothes until it arrived, and had been waiting by my side at the hospital for three days without informing my parents. Statements were taken. The most intimate detail was included in the forensic report, but no one else found out. My cousin didn't ask me anything. After I was discharged from the hospital, we called my parents from the village. They and those who heard about the incident believed that I fell into depression and attempted suicide because of our separation shortly before the wedding. I didn't deny it.

In that moment, when I was glad that I was alive, a new life began for me. Nothing would be the same any more. This was my life. I wouldn't allow myself to leave it behind. I would give justice to staying alive by cherishing every moment, by not letting it be taken away from me again...

I never saw him again. I heard the news about him involuntarily. I listened as if they were talking about a stranger. One day, they said he had died. It was a car accident. He was alone. He got trapped in the car. They said he died from blood loss while waiting for an ambulance. Trapped in the car...

I tried to form a few sentences; I think I succeeded. But I don't know how meaningful they were. I had to leave there as soon as possible. I needed to be alone first. I would figure out the rest later. When I got up, she got up too. I paid the bill. We hurriedly said our goodbyes at the café door. I had just started working when she called me on the phone. "I fooled you, didn't I... Turns out I'm good at writing stories, huh?" I expected her to say that. But she didn't. Her voice was cheerful. She said she felt free as a bird. "It's as if I've been trapped all these years while not telling anyone about what happened. With tons of weight on my wings or wings made of brass... It's as if I pulled out a dark magic from within me. Now I feel as light as a feather," she said.

It was at that moment that I lost control. "Because you passed that curse onto me. So how will I escape?" I shouted.

Without hesitation and quite calmly, she answered. "You write, that's about all."

It was definitely a story worth writing. She felt the relief of finally telling someone after all those years. Maybe writing was the only way for me to escape the burden of knowing. Before ending the call, I said, "Then tell the end of the story." Her soft voice had acquired a cheerful tone.

I have already told my happy-ending. As for what happened next, let me tell you. I confronted myself, and I emerged stronger from this chaos. The greatest punishment for him was my nonchalance. I would punish him with my happiness, with my life. By giving myself the world... I graduated from university with this determination. I became an advertiser. The man I met at work, who made me experience true love all these years, patiently healed my last wound without knowing the cause. I was ready for marriage. I've been married for a month now. I love my husband very much; his laughter spoils me.

When I hung up the phone, I knew I would write her story. It was living proof that no matter how many times and from how high we fall, we can stand up again, and that we can hold onto life once more. Now I understand what she meant when she said that writing can even save lives.

Luminary Water

Yasemin was a remarkable and ambitious young woman in the early stages of her career in English Literature. If you were to ask her colleagues, her ambition could be interpreted as intimidating. She had started attending international conferences at a very early stage. Awards, papers, book chapters... While her peers were still figuring out "who am I?" she had long since learned, even declared, who she was. She had numerous international experiences and a special interest in England. Her most recent research had been about Sylvia Plath, which brought her to England two years ago. The three-month period covered Cambridge, where the poet had studied on a scholarship, North Tawton, where she lived with her husband and children, and London, where she settled alone after the divorce and ended her life.

When she was already a student, Yasemin had devoured Sylvia Plath's poems, novels, and stories. She was well aware of the urban legend who eventually had committed suicide, which only fueled her curiosity. One quote deeply affected her: "Perhaps when we find ourselves wanting everything, it is because we are dangerously close to wanting nothing." She thought that Sylvia Plath portrayed consumer society and especially the idea of eventual depletion in a striking way, and she made this perspective the backbone of her work. Her influential conference paper soon turned into an article.

This time, she chose another city: Bristol. And there was a

reason behind this choice, of course. It had only been a few days since she arrived in the city. After leaving her belongings in the rented room provided by the university, she prioritized exploring the city. Since she didn't know anyone, she was going to wander around alone. Around noon that day, she found herself on a hill not too far from the center of Bristol, where tourists could see the Clifton Suspension Bridge, often referred to as "the greatest bridge ever built of stone." Little she knew that this moment would turn into an internal reckoning. If she had known, would she have fled? Most likely. After a long walk, she felt the need to catch her breath, and she unknowingly settled on a bench, about to embark on an inner journey. In a place like this, amidst the beauty of nature, contemplating such a magnificent structure felt like a paradox. Under the bridge flowed a large river: the River Avon. The water was murky, just like her mind, but she wasn't concerned about it at that moment. In the past, she would have disliked this situation, as her fondest memories of rivers were about dipping her bare feet into clear waters. Now, those memories were too distant to recall.

While standing on the bridge, she closed her eyes and held onto the railings. Completely made of stone and suspended by thick steel cables, the bridge was remarkably sturdy. Yet, curiously, it seemed affected by the frailty of the people passing between its two ends. The vibrations caused by the passing cars spread through Yasemin's entire being, making her feel like a part of a larger whole. She even noticed that the wind's howling caused the bridge to sway slightly. She had to surrender herself to this sense of integration with her eyes closed. Even though she had no intention of moving her arm earlier, suddenly she felt a vitality and movement that extended to the furthest points of her body, which felt like a warning to her. Without objecting to its guidance, she allowed her steps to lead her away from the bridge and bring her to the bench where she was now sitting. Shortly after, a woman came and sat next to her casually. Yasemin, unable to keep up with the speed of her thoughts, was unaware of how long she had been sitting there, gazing at the bridge. She found herself in moments when she fully embraced the loneliness she had recently come to accept, loneliness that filled her inside and suffocated her breath. She preferred being physically alone, which made the presence of this woman cause even more discomfort than it would at any other time.

Looking back, it might be easier to reinterpret the events in the order they happened, but she couldn't do that at the time. She couldn't see the meaning in every detail. Besides, even if she could, what business did she have being there? The woman also watched the bridge for a while. Just when Yasemin thought, *At least the silence remains,* she heard the woman's voice: "Would you like some gum?" Yasemin wondered if she misheard; the woman continued, "Strawberry and watermelon, my favorites."

At that moment, the woman had already put two pieces of gum into her mouth and started chewing. The scent of strawberry and watermelon blending into something else reached Yasemin with the woman's warm breath. It reminded her of the half-green, half-red strawberries they used to grow in a pot with her brother during her childhood. They were within arm's reach, but her mother's voice saying, "Don't eat those, they're not edible," turned her attention to the other side of the bridge. The scent of strawberry and watermelon had passed. She looked toward the woman. However, she was no longer looking at Yasemin. She was speaking aloud, with her mouth full of gum, and the words were escaping through her teeth, talking about the bridge. "Did you know that jumping off this bridge used to be quite trendy for suicide?" the woman said. Yasemin was startled. The woman had no intention of stopping; she continued, "In the early years, a twenty-two-year-old woman threw herself into the void, but when her skirt opened like a parachute, she couldn't avoid landing softly in the river. She lived until she was eighty."

Yasemin had no intention of responding, at least not out loud. She could speak to herself inside her mind. Of course, she had heard about the bridge's notoriety. She even thought about the Bosphorus Bridge in Istanbul. But she saw the incidents there as a spectacle mostly created by people seeking attention. She believed that those who were truly determined, silently and discreetly jumping and achieving their goals, went unnoticed because such incidents didn't make the news. Before traveling, it had been her habit for years to research the cities. At this time, she wasn't in a sightseeing or knowledge-seeking mood. Nevertheless, she had skimmed through a few books. Among them, this bridge had caught her attention. One book mentioned that although raising the bridge railings seemed to be an effective measure twenty years ago, suicide attempts still continued to yield results.

She decided to come to Bristol. After choosing this small city as her destination, she began researching English writers associated with it. She didn't know of any famous poet or writer connected to this city that would particularly interest her. But she could find one. It was easy to do so now. She Googled it. Typing in "Bristol, poet, poem, writer, and novel" brought up Iris Murdoch's name. When she saw this name at the top of the search results, she was startled. Her path coinciding with another "bird woman" at this exact point both surprised and frightened her. She remembered what she had read in a newspaper article: "Some women are uncatchable, unstoppable, and can't belong to anyone. They don't even belong to themselves; it's a complicated matter. You can only get close to those women, and if you catch and stop them, make them yours... they just die."

Yasemin knew Iris Murdoch as a literature scholar from Oxford. Murdoch had taught philosophy classes there for many years and also wrote her books there. Due to Alzheimer's disease, as she lost her words, she described this condition as being in a "very bad, silent, and dark place," unable even to remember the titles of her books, she was there "slowed down and stopped." According to the new information Yasemin learned from internet sites, Iris's childhood and adolescence were spent in Bristol. Thus, Yasemin found a reason to start her research from there. She quickly made the necessary arrangements, and there she was.

Did the woman sitting next to her know all this? As she pondered this, she realized that the woman was still talking. The voice she began to hear again was still about the bridge. Suddenly, she heard a piece of information that was not among the things she had read. "They are volunteers; they call themselves Samaritans. They placed the phone booths at both ends of the bridge. Someone is there on the phone twenty-four hours a day, seven days a week, can you imagine? They've written it in big letters: 'Talk to us. Night or day, anytime!' I don't know if they did ever succeed. What can you say to someone who wants to destroy themselves? Sometimes, I wonder what I would say if I were in that situation." At this moment, Yasemin noticed that she was starting to smell the scent of strawberry and watermelon combination again. At the same time, a silly thought came to her mind: *How long does the smell last? I wonder what brand of gum it is.* It was as if she would buy that gum from the first store she saw.

The woman, with eyes that indicated she was expecting an

answer, asked, "Have you ever thought about it?" Yasemin couldn't immediately grasp that the question was about what could be said to dissuade someone from suicide. Luckily, the woman continued without waiting for an answer, "If you say something, that person will live... I wish it were possible..."

Yasemin realized that there would be no dialog with the woman. The thoughts rushing into her mind prevented it. *Who were these volunteers? Such a job couldn't be done without the thought of saving another person's life becoming an obsession. When that person had given up their life, what impulse would stand against this will? I wonder if they really succeed.* Then that question began to turn in Yasemin's mind: *What do they say to persuade someone to choose life?*

When she got up from the bench, she didn't look to see if the woman was still there. She started walking without a plan; she didn't even know where she was going. She was surprised when she reached the beginning of the bridge. Nevertheless, she continued walking without stopping. When she noticed that there were no car noises this time as she had heard when she first crossed the bridge, she saw that the bridge was closed to traffic. Furthermore, it was swaying much more than she had felt before. She heard a short whistle and a police officer who came to her and blocked her way told her that pedestrian crossings on the bridge were also blocked. She was one of the few people stopped, and the police politely explained to this small group: "The wind has become very strong, and as it may be dangerous, this precaution has been taken. This is the first time something like this has happened, but don't worry; according to the information from the meteorology, it will be short."

When Yasemin learned that they were witnessing a historical event, she murmured, "Let's write today's date somewhere; February 12, 2014. Moreover, it's my thirtieth birthday…"

At that moment, Yasemin's eyes fell on the telephone booth. Being before the restricted zone meant she could go there. She jingled the coins in her pocket. She headed toward the phone. The writing the woman mentioned was still there. The phone number to be called was written on the same sign, hung on the stonewall. It was stated just below that the call was free. She stood still inside the booth for a while. She picked up the receiver with her left hand. She stroked the cord with her right fingers a few times. Then she dialed the numbers given. She wondered how many times it would ring before someone answered. Immediately after that, she thought about how only the most absurd questions came to her mind and raised the corner of her lips with a slightly contemptuous expression.

The male voice on the other end answered without the phone even ringing. Yasemin was caught off guard. Actually, she didn't know what kind of preparation she could make. Even if she had time to think about what to say to someone she had never met in a language other than her native language, she might not be able to do it; especially, considering the subject she would talk about… The male voice on the other end started talking with a warm *"hello"* as if it were a natural phone call between two acquaintances. Then he said his name, *"I'm Andrew."* Without pausing, he added, *"I'm glad you called."*

Yasemin fell silent, not because she didn't know what to say this time, but because she thought she didn't want to respond to this affected politeness. Since she first learned of their existence, she had doubts about the sincerity of these people. She didn't find it very convincing that the actions of this group calling themselves volunteers were merely a well-intentioned effort to keep callers in life. They must have a hidden agenda. She thought to herself, *He's glad I called, pfff. What's it to you? What's this eagerness to dissuade a person you don't know, whose circumstances you don't know, and whose pains you can't understand?* Then a thought crossed her mind, which she would later find absurd: *What do they do if someone calls when they go to the bathroom, to avoid missing the call?*

During Yasemin's silence, Andrew also remained silent. It was an expectation arising from accepting that the connection established was only to continue if she wanted it; it was good for Yasemin. She felt relieved when she thought she had control. She could start talking now.

"*Actually, I called out of mere curiosity. I didn't want to tie up the line; I might be preventing someone who truly needs it from calling you right now. The idea that you believe you can dissuade a determined person from committing suicide seems unrealistic to me. I was wondering about the method you use.*"

"*There are multiple lines, and if needed, additional calls can be directed to my friends' phones. Some days, we don't receive any calls, while on others, we get a maximum of two calls. After all, no one dials our number just for the sake of it.*"

"*If you don't mind, I have a question to ask.*"

"*Of course, go ahead. I'd be glad to answer if it's something I can.*"

Yasemin thought to herself, *Oh, these butterfly-of-love mannerisms are going to kill me!* Then, she realized the irony in what she just said. If Andrew caused someone's death, he probably wouldn't recover from it.

"*How do you start the conversation? Do you initiate the subject? Is it discussed indirectly or directly?*"

"*Each conversation flows differently. It seems to be directed* based on the person's needs, but more often, the level of determination determines the direction of the conversation."

"Actually, there is no such situation, but let's say I called to ask for help. What would be your approach?"

"I would expect you to tell your story. If the silence becomes too prolonged or if nothing substantial is said even when spoken, that also has a meaning. The person responding to our call eventually gets to the main issue."

"I thought about it, and it would have been better if you started by asking what caused the severing of their connection with life."

"What would your response be to such a question?"

Yasemin paused. She felt like she was leading herself into a trap. Then, she thought with a slight raise of her right eyebrow. She had to admit that Andrew made a good move. No matter how good he was, he wouldn't be able to trap her. She certainly wouldn't discuss such a personal matter with a stranger, especially one whose name and face she didn't even know. However, she had to acknowledge that she might share it with a stranger, especially one whose name and face she didn't even know.

Continuing the conversation, she wanted to reiterate the last question, "What would my response be to such a question?" At that moment, she realized something. She had been feeling that her connection with life was weakening for a long time, but she had never questioned the reason behind it. She needed to delve into her deepest thoughts. Sweeping things under the rug wouldn't be enough; she had to bring to light the dirt she had buried under the concrete she poured into the hole she dug under the carpet. It was laborious.

The easiest thing was to just go on living. She had done it

many times. Every time, after a few months of a depressive state, she managed to cling to a new wave of joy and come out of it. When the story of the Little Match Girl came to her mind, she initially thought it was just one of those random thoughts that popped into her head. *Did it have any meaning or not? After all, wasn't the little girl who tried to warm herself on a matchstick and was found dead among the scattered matchsticks at the end of the story?* It sent shivers down her spine.

Perhaps the time had come for her to question some things. How much longer could she postpone it? She should start by thinking about the most recent event she experienced. As she went back, she started to feel that some things would become clearer in her mind. But she couldn't do it over the phone. Suddenly, she remembered Andrew, silently waiting on the other end of the line. In fact, she wanted to talk to him again. But maybe later…

"Andrew, if I hang up now and call you later, will you be there?"

"*Of course, I told you, this is not a huge call center. I'm alone on this shift. So, I'll be the one to answer every time the phone rings until morning. Will you really come back?*"

"*That's the plan. I'm in a situation I can't explain right now. Don't get me wrong; it's not because I don't trust you. I just can't fully comprehend it yet. Something inside me has stirred, like the first domino has fallen, and others will follow one by one; I can feel it. In fact, this might be the last domino; maybe they will all stand up again. Thus, I will stand up. Do you understand?*"

"*I can't say I fully understand, but I want you to know that what you're saying makes sense. Also, I want you to be aware of the strength I perceive in your voice. It's a sign that you will find the right path within yourself. I'll be waiting for you to call again."*

Yasemin hung up the receiver. She couldn't move. Inside the telephone booth, she sat on the floor, surrounded by a cloud. Her vision was closed to anyone but herself. And so she drifted into thoughts. She could start by describing her current state of mind. She had recently ended a long-term relationship. Actually, she had wanted it to end for a while, but she couldn't bring herself to tell her partner. Finally, with the feeling that the knife was at her throat, she attempted to put an end to it. And this wasn't the first time either. She had a few experiences that led her to believe in the discourse that love expires in three years. It was as if there had been a curse on her relationships since her youth. They would start with great enthusiasm and continue that way for a while. Then, she would withdraw herself in the turbulence of her own confusion. Without showing it to the other person, she would try to revive the feeling. In fact, she succeeded a few times in rejuvenating it. Then the inevitable end would come. It was always abrupt. "It's over," she would say, like a child throwing a tantrum. "It's none of my business; it's over!" So far, she hadn't returned from this decision. She saw the other person's acceptance of her one-sided breakup as an opportunity. This way, she could avoid being questioned by the person she left or herself. But how long could this continue?

Yes, leaving had always been easy for her. Still, endings always left a deep ache within her. She attributed this to her failures in love. Her rock bottom coincided with these times, just like it was happening now. After a time of feeling cold and trembling inside, she would light a new match. A match? Ah, the subconscious. Indeed, the feeling created by the thrown matchsticks, just before burning her fingers, beautifully defined the moments of separation. This would repeat until all the matches in the box were used. Now, since she was wandering around here, she must have reached the bottom of the box. If this was going to continue like this, she felt she couldn't take it anymore. She couldn't start again. She feared the outcome would be the same. She was even certain of it, without leaving room for doubt. Suddenly, she remembered a concept she had heard before: the test of life. Everyone had a test of life. It was a test that kept coming back until it was passed; tests that sought the same answer in different conditions with different people. Knots that needed to be untangled and understood about ourselves, so we could continue on our way.

If there really was such a test that poisoned her life, she needed to find out what it was. She had begun to see that these painful relationships followed a similar cycle. The details unnoticed while she was in them were clearly exposed when she looked at them from a distance. She thought that her distance from where she lived influenced this. She was looking at the whole picture from afar and saw striking similarities in the compositions that came together. It surprised her that there was not a single visual that disrupted the integrity. How was this possible when she felt so shattered inside?

Slowly, she began to perceive the common thread that created this harmony. The lovers in these relationships were all married. Living far away from Yasemin was also a common characteristic. This made it difficult for them to meet frequently. They were husbands who honestly stated from the beginning that they were unhappy in their marriages but couldn't end them due to social pressure, years of habit, or a sense of gratitude for the years they had endured together. It seemed to be the unchanging rule of their relationships. And then, there was the admiration and even love they felt for Yasemin from their first meeting. Some had even called it the joy of life, claiming that Yasemin turned their winter into spring. It was enough for them to be convinced. And just when she said, "Never again," she found herself in such a relationship. The consequence was love. Her favorite feeling...

When she was in love, it was as if her heart proclaimed that it would never stop beating. Like immortality. Moreover, she developed a dependency on the attention she received. If the dosage didn't increase gradually, problems would arise. However, the person she was with embraced her with enthusiasm, never diminishing but always increasing their interest. Yasemin wasn't surprised by this; she thought she deserved to be loved with such passion. Even during the most intense depressive periods, she never felt worthless. She was nourished by the souls saying she had brought them back to life. Thus, she experienced an indescribable fulfillment.

She hadn't asked any of her partners to divorce and be with her only. It had never crossed her mind. In fact, when she thought about it, she could even say that she was afraid of it. Maybe because she knew deep down that a lifetime destined for such a relationship might be possible. If her feelings ever faded away, she would be burdened with the responsibility of breaking someone's life because of her. Whenever she said, "It's over," the other person accepting it as an inevitable end made things much easier. These reactions were now more understandable for Yasemin. After all, the lovers who hadn't made any promises, maybe hadn't even considered it, found comfort in the idea of "thank goodness, I didn't disrupt my life for this relationship" instead of being devastated after the breakup. Now, he was resting and continuing on their way, cooled off in an oasis. The love they once found in Yasemin had made them happy with memories without any risks.

In the beginning of her last affair, everything had happened in the same order as before. There were no promises, and once again, after three years, Yasemin had seen her enthusiasm fade away. The only difference was that this time she felt a pressure to question what was happening in her subconscious. The man who had been telling Yasemin for years that her happiness was his happiness was now making all sorts of accusations to sow the seeds of guilt in her soul. He insulted her, threw threats, and blamed her the most. Yet both seemed to have accepted that they would go as far as the relationship could take them. When one side did not want to see that they were not going any further, they became irritable and even regretted the beautiful memories. Yasemin couldn't find any solution other than escaping. It was what she did best. She thought coming to a distant city would make it possible. She was just beginning to think that she was running away to get caught. Seeing all this had not been of much benefit to Yasemin. It couldn't be expected to have a healing effect, especially on her. Yes, if there really was such a thing as the test of life, she had found it for herself. The cyclical nature of what had happened made this very clear. But the more important part remained unsolved. Why did she have to take this test multiple times?

    She was not aware of how much time she had spent sitting on the floor of the phone booth. But feeling her crossed legs numb indicated that a long time had passed. Using the iron handles fixed to the walls on both sides, she pulled herself up and stood. Both her feet were tingling. She remembered liking this feeling when she was a child. She couldn't understand what was happening, but she found it strangely enjoyable to feel as if hundreds of needles were pricking her feet without causing too much pain. She would press her feet harder on the ground. When the needles had gone all the way into her feet, she believed the pain would pass. She did it again. It worked once more. Now she could walk. But which way to go?

Yasemin reached the railing of the bridge and started to watch the Aron River. It was uncertain whether it was flowing or not. There was no noticeable movement in its waters. Perhaps that was why it looked murky. She noticed a footpath leading down the opposite slope. She walked slowly toward that direction on the bridge, which was now open to traffic. Numerous cars were struggling to move forward, indicating that there had been quite a build-up while waiting for the wind to calm down. It even made Yasemin think that the calm and patient English people honking their horns impatiently meant the waiting period was quite long.

As soon as she descended the path, she was by the riverbank. She took a deep breath. Being by the water always relaxed her. The water looked dark green up close, but it didn't appear dirty. It was evident that even the edges were deep. For centuries, it had been used for the entry and exit of large merchant ships and even warships to the Bristol Harbor, and it was very suitable for the safety of these passages. She walked along the river for a while. This was the second stage of her plan. She would try to find out why she was always trapped in the same cycle and couldn't escape it. She could imagine that it would be a more difficult process than before. Since it had not caught her attention until now, there must be some deeply buried experience that needed to be pulled out from the layers of oblivion. It might be a feeling she needed to unearth. Difficult as it may be, she had to try; after all, she couldn't give up when she was so close.

What did Andrew say? "I sense strength in your voice." Who knows how many people especially those private phone conversations he had turned him into an expert on reading voices. She wanted him to be right. She remembered the soft determination in his voice. He was in the right tone to give her strength. She wanted to call him right away, but she hadn't finished what she needed to do yet.

There were no benches by the riverbank, so she found a slightly elevated stone to sit on. Plump seagulls were flying in the sky, squawking loudly. They were a crowd. Two of them, especially, separated from the flock and circled above Yasemin's head. They looked cheerful. Whenever she went to new places, Yasemin would interpret seagulls for fortune-telling. If the first seagull she saw was alone, it would spoil her mood. She would assume the atmosphere for the days she would spend there had already been determined. She hadn't been wrong before, in fact. What should she attribute this enthusiastic flock of seagulls to? And what about those two seagulls?

A melody played in her ears. It was coming from a distance. It was difficult to identify which song it was. But she realized it was getting closer. The sound was becoming clearer. She turned around and saw two young girls coming toward her. One of them was playing a song on her phone to her friend. They were walking with the liveliness of youth, laughing. When they joined in the chorus, the song became even more audible: "And my heart belongs to my daddy. *Dadada dadada dadada…*" Yasemin had first heard this song from Marilyn Monroe. Though the movie "Let's Make Love" was a commercial failure, this song had reached the top. Many singers sang it before and after, but what came to Yasemin's mind was Marilyn's mischievous, childlike appearance, combined with her sexy image. Yasemin began to hum the song as well. "Yes, my heart belongs to my daddy, So I simply couldn't be bad."

Suddenly, something happened. As Yasemin gazed at the dark green waters of the Aron River, a scene began to ripple on the surface. Her father was there. All alone; looking sad. Yes, yes, he was definitely unhappy. She couldn't remember ever seeing him like this. When was it, certainly? Then the scene changed. It was as if the camera turned to the other side. She saw herself as a little child with her mother. She must have been around four or five years old. It was probably winter because she was wearing a coat that was too big for her. She also had a small scarf tied around her head. She was holding her mother's left hand, who was also wearing a coat and a scarf. They resembled each other. Her mother had a suitcase in her right hand. They are about to leave. Not like going on a trip.

Her father's image appears again. He stands still as if he might shatter if touched. After these images, Yasemin remembered a forgotten event, and even a few more events that followed. Her mother had taken Yasemin along when she left her father. Yasemin never wanted to go, but she couldn't say anything. She had gotten used to yielding to the warnings of "Don't meddle in the affairs of adults!" at that young age. She couldn't recall how long it took for her father to come and get them from her grandmother's house. Once they were back in their own house, she ran to her room. Her toys were right where she left them. No other children had come to play, it seemed. Her mother had mentioned something like that. Thinking about other kids taking her place made Yasemin feel sad. Fortunately, there was no one else. Their home was theirs again, just the three of them.

The relief she felt at that moment didn't last long. Her parents were so unhappy that when they started fighting, little Yasemin didn't know where to escape. She fell sick often, and her mother would get angry, blaming it on her. Everything was somehow her fault. She expected her father to pay attention to her, but he never came near. She began to think that she had upset him. Clearly, his unhappiness was caused by Yasemin. When she grew a bit older, she remembered constantly thinking that she wished her parents would separate. But they didn't. However, the fights eventually stopped for a while. Unaware of the consequences, she was tossed around by her own teenage tensions. It was impossible to see what was going on at home. Then she passed the university entrance exam and went to another city, gradually distancing herself from her family, just as she wanted.

As she was searching for answers by the river, the song she heard and the imaginary scene she saw on the river's surface triggered her to revisit all these memories. Under different circumstances, she might not have felt the same emotion, but at that moment, she felt her perception was very clear. The connection between all these things became clear. It almost materialized. The lovers who couldn't find the strength to escape from their unhappy marriages were actually her father. So, she had always consoled her father. Yasemin was aware of how important a path she had taken in her personal history. However, she didn't feel any lightness inside yet. But she was certain it would come. The domino pieces had fallen just as she predicted, one by one. Now it was her turn to stand up. One last move... She felt she already knew what it was.

She stood up from the stone she was sitting on. Facing the river with her entire body, she spread her arms wide. She leaned forward slightly. She shouted as if vomiting: "It's over now, Dad! If you wanted happiness, you would have gone after it. I am not responsible for your cowardice. Why did you turn a blind eye to how I felt? You were the one who couldn't leave, just like the others. You have a thousand excuses. To hell with you! I wish you had taken care of your own happiness and been a model for me. I won't give up just because you couldn't do it. I just want to be happy, Dad; is that too much to ask? I won't fail the same test again. You can celebrate my graduation. I really want you to find peace in the end, but there is nothing I can do about that. I am only responsible for myself. So are you. Do you understand?"

She felt her insides empty. She dropped to her knees and closed her eyes. She took deep breaths for a while, and then her breath calmed. Lines from Sylvia Plath's "Daddy" poem came to her mind.

She wanted to make an optimistic choice. Two new lines spilled from her lips, *"The reward for being understood is to understand / As one is born, the other dies."*

As she was about to get up, she noticed a few small daisies among the grass. She picked them and tucked them into her light chestnut hair. Just randomly... She knew where she was going. She stumbled along the path, her imagination creating a melody from the jingling bells around the necks of mountain goats. She crossed the bridge again. She was glad to see the phone booth empty. She took the receiver in her left hand and coiled the cord around her right hand a few times. She dialed the same number. As she pressed the last digit, she took a deep breath and held it. Andrew's warm greeting greeted her as the phone answered, and she let out her breath slowly.

"Andrew, it's me, Yasemin!"
"I'm glad you called."
"Me too!"
"How are you?"
"I'm good, very good."

"I'm really glad to hear that."

"Can you stop with the pleasantries? I want us to talk honestly."

"OK... But first, I need to ask something personal. It's important."

Yasemin was surprised. What important and personal thing could Andrew want to know about her? What was she ready to share with him, and to what extent? Could she share things she hadn't spoken to anyone else about until then?

"I'm waiting for your answer. Did you call this number to give yourself a chance before committing suicide?"

"I thought you couldn't ask that question directly."

"Don't do that. I can easily tell you're not feeling that way right now. It's not a 'professional' conversation anymore. That's quite clear. But I couldn't decide whether that was your intention during our first call. I needed to know."

"I'm sorry, Andrew. I didn't mean to put you in an awkward position. I'm just feeling a great excitement inside; the arrogance of it. I'm really sorry. As for your question, no, it wasn't a pre-suicide meeting. In fact, I never crossed that thought in my mind, even during my worst times. I might have thought, 'It would be better if I were dead,' but the idea of attempting was always out of the question. And this time, too..."

"That relieves me. Do you know why? If you had called for help, I wouldn't have been able to ask you the question I'm about to ask."

"There are so many questions... Fortunately, today is my 'day of answers.'"

"Will you meet me for a coffee?"

Yasemin wasn't expecting this question. If they didn't have a professional meeting, she could interpret their encounter differently. She thought about it. Yes, she wanted to be friends with Andrew. She felt great excitement about getting to know him, introducing herself to him, enjoying the pleasure of friendship with him, and, if feelings turned into love, then experiencing that to the fullest. This time would be different. The voice inside her said so. She smiled, thinking that she had not regretted listening to that voice all day. There was one last security measure.

"First, you answer me. Are you married?"

At the Table

I found the restaurant easily. "Turn left after you exit the meeting hall, follow the road up a slight slope," they had told me. "There is a shop selling local sweets on the corner. After you pass it, right across from it, there is the restaurant, its name written on a ceramic sign. You cannot miss it."

The local sweets shop appeared right in front of me, just as they had described, yet I could not walk past its window. There were colorful fruits placed on plates, shimmering in the light. Rows of shelves filled with plates, each for a different type of fruit, were arranged in the window. Such vivid colors they had. These sweets, *frutta Martonara*, sold here must be the ones described as the specialty of Sicily by those who tasted them as they licked their lips.

I entered the sweets shop right away. If this was in my town, they would have handed me one to taste. Not here of course... and I was hesitant to ask. *I'd better pick the ones I liked the most, in a medium size paper bag,* I thought. There is a reason why I mentioned lemon and strawberry before; they are my favorite flavors. I picked a few of these immediately and brought them close to my nose. Not sure why I expected them to smell. They looked so real, I guess. They didn't smell of anything specific. The peach looked fuzzy, just like the strawberry had little black spots on it, and the little watermelon slice had seeds. I put a few of these as well in my paper bag and I was done. I could have easily carried on, but I thought to myself, *Let me just try these, and if I enjoy them, then there is still tomorrow.* I left the shop after getting my change and couldn't resist any longer. So, I stuck one of the strawberries in my mouth there and then. What an unexpected taste it was. I was already looking forward to going back to my room after dinner, so I could continue to eat the rest of it.

Shortly ahead, I found the restaurant; I entered by pushing its glass door. It was an authentic place, made ready for Christmas with the decorations. On top of the wide bar to my right, there were glass jars full of cookies, and on the counter behind the bar, a series of coffee machines were neatly arranged. If I hadn't noticed the narrow archway to the restaurant side, I would have thought that I had entered a coffee shop by mistake.

I rushed past the stove, which was partially blocking the already narrow entrance, as the heat from it brushed my legs. The large rectangular table in the middle was full of people. Apparently, everyone had taken their place while I was lingering in the sweets shop. I gazed at some of the faces I knew with a slightly upset look, as if to ask why they hadn't saved a place for me, but they didn't notice. They were all engaged in their own deep conversations about who knows what. Even the small round tables, which looked like satellites that were surrounding the large one in the middle, were almost completely full. So, I grabbed a chair by a round table that was nearest to me and asked the people whom I had only said hello to on a few occasions, "Is this free? May I sit here?" I took my seat quickly at their approving noises. I was worried about giving an impression to others of not being welcomed by my friends in the room by standing for long. People sitting at the table greeted me with polite words.

We were at a small gathering of a group of doctors with

similar areas of interest. Two or at most five people from the same country were invited. In this meeting, bringing experienced people and new starters together, the objective was not to give lectures but to share knowledge of the areas that only a small number of people across the world were interested in.

Being invited to this meeting, which had given me a sense of exclusivity, had taken an even more special meaning when I saw where it was going to take place. It was in a medieval mountain village in Sicily, a place in which we could witness the foggy clouds descending on us, creating a magical view as we felt the harsh cold of winter in our bones. What attracted me the most were the rocky spots with their strong winds where we could see the open seas from above.

On the other hand, this meeting was like an unequaled feast from a scientific point of view. It allowed for acquaintances, yet I expected that it would be difficult to continue these connections once we returned to the real world afterward. When we meet again in larger crowds, it would be hard to reform these close interactions. Still, without a doubt, when we returned to our jobs across different parts of the world, the impressions of this special meeting would stay with us.

Neither these meetings nor the times when we sang together around the piano at night were creating opportunities for deep conversations. Only those who happened to sit around the same table for meals had the chance to take their relationship a few steps further.

The wooden chair next to me was empty. There was a coat left casually on its back, giving the impression that someone had been sitting there but had to leave urgently. I was not mistaken. A short while later, a young man was walking toward us as he came off the phone. He came and sat in his seat after neatening his coat on the chair. He must have not noticed that I had joined the crowd, as he didn't greet me. He seemed somewhat preoccupied. We soon discovered why. Another man at the table, about the same age as him, looked at the man sitting next to me and asked, "What's up, Phillip? I hope it wasn't bad news. Your face had such an expression when you saw the name on the phone, it made me really curious. Then you went outside in this cold to take the call and stayed there for so long."

Phillip took a deep breath and let it out gently, and replied, "Actually, I don't think you could say bad news. My childhood friend is having a divorce. It was his choice. It's been fifteen days since he picked up his coat and left the house to move into a hotel room. Now that Christmas is approaching, the thought of being away from his kids at Christmas for the first time is dawning on him. So, I feel it is my duty to console him."

"Doesn't he know that you are abroad for a meeting? It's kind of selfish, isn't it?"

"I don't see it that way. He has always been there for me during hard times."

"That's all very well, but he must have thought long and hard before taking action. People should face the consequences of their choices."

The conversation was taking place as a dialog with the person who asked the first question. We were all listening to them. The man, who I figured was called Phillip, continued, "He doesn't regret his decision. It is just that the consequences regarding his children are making him sad. He is not expecting me to find a solution, he just wants me to listen. That's all I can do, anyway. I keep telling him that it'll all sort itself out and that this is the toughest period. Hoping that it'll have more impact than what he is telling himself..."

"That's what I always say; time is the cure for everything..."

As the people around the table, we were just listening. We couldn't make any comments since we didn't know the subject. Someone had better explain as I was getting weary of both not being able to join in with the conversation, and not really knowing what they were talking about. Phillip, almost as though he had sensed that we were feeling this way, turned to us and gave a brief summary. His childhood friend is a very rich plastic surgeon. "A multimillionaire," he said. There was some laughter in the group, and comments were made about him not going to be alone for long.

"Many times, 'I would willingly give away all my money if I could just be happy,' he told me," Phillip said, in a very serious manner, ending the laughter as if it was cut with a knife. Then Phillip continued to explain; a controlling wife, who wants to decide everything on her own, a personality who is still not satisfied with the outcomes and blaming the person, but above all jealous to the point of illness. A husband, who up and leaves when push comes to shove, and without any regrets, not even for one second. He is not considering going back, ever. He only wants to make sure that his relationship with the kids is back on track. He is worried that his wife may not be very cooperative during this period of reconciliation, which she has shown signs of based on his experience so far.

A middle-aged man who was among the listeners took the scene as these were being told. I didn't know his name since no one had addressed him by it, but I found it appropriate to name him the Silent Cowboy in my mind. This was the only time the Silent Cowboy had spoken throughout the whole dinner.

"People make mistakes when they are young. I am divorced as well. It's been almost ten years. When people are young, they neglect their partners—work, trips, and idol times spent with friends and—they don't realize that they break the heart of the one waiting for them at home. Then you are left all alone. It was tough, really tough for me. Yet I think your friend is right; the most important part of it is to keep the relationship with the children in place. My son was fourteen years old when we got divorced. I was lucky to have his custody. I happen to think that my ex-wife had left him to me so that he would be a burden to me. However, this led to us bonding as father and son and eventually, our relationship grew stronger." The Silent Cowboy bowed his head down after he told this. It was as if he was revisiting those times and reliving them. It was clear that he was not waiting for a comment and so we did not make any.

At that moment, the man who had first called out to Phillip —well, let's call him the Initiator—started talking. He was talking to us, but he had a reluctant look, if you ask me. "Well, my share of the exam was not so easy, either. Our little daughter is one year old now. If I could have the first six months erased from my memory, I would. Science has advanced so far, but they just can't do that yet. Erasing all unwanted memories, for good... How wonderful would that be, right? Actually, I recall having watched a movie like this, Eternal Sunshine of the Spotless Mind. A girl who had broken up with her boyfriend goes to a specialist place to get their time together, and everything she knows about him erased from her memory."

This was one of my favorite films. It was translated into Turkish as "Start from Scratch." I had thought so much about the details of the movie after watching it. In fact, I had watched it over and over again and, each time, I had spotted a different aspect. There were times I had said, *"What a great idea,"* and other times, *"It can't do any good. Everything we live through is precious,*" to myself. This was a good chance to jump into the discussion. I did not miss it.

"I know that movie. It was the girl who had her memories erased first. And then the boy, who thinks that this girl who used to be his girlfriend, pretends to not know him intentionally, but once he finds out the truth, he decides to do the same, as some kind of revenge. When the removal procedure starts, he regrets what he is doing and tries to run away. That part struck me the most. He tries to hide among his most embarrassing childhood memories, ones that he hasn't shared to be erased. After having seen this film, I often wondered whether we would continue to be ourselves if we had some of our memories removed."

I had managed to join the discussion and so had taken the first step to be part of the group. Still, my attempt to do that must have been seen as stealing his part, as it was not appreciated by the Initiator. He continued where he had left off as if he had not heard what I said, in order not to let the topic drift away.

"When my wife wanted to take a longer leave after our second daughter was born, to stay with her and our elder daughter who was two and a half years old, I told her that we could arrange this. I realized that she was getting exhausted even though she was on leave, and even when our daughter was two months old, and suggested that we find a helper who could come every day. She was not ready to delegate any responsibility to anyone. Not even to me. She wanted to take care of the girls on her own and this had suited me well, too. I was extremely busy at work; since I was invited to meetings as a speaker one after the other, my days at the hospital were even busier than I was used to. My agenda was filled with ever-growing 'to-do' lists. I used to go home very late, almost half asleep. I would head upstairs to take a short nap in the rocking chair, to the sounds of creaking as it rocked, until the dinner table was ready, while my wife would be rushing around at her own pace. I was having a good time at home, without thinking even once about how she had managed to do all these things with two children."

Sounds of disapproval from one of the women at the table disrupted this monologue. She was chubby, short, casual-looking, and short-haired—I thought just short enough, so she didn't have to comb it—brunette, in her thirties. I figured she was angry, from the deep crease between her thick eyebrows and her waving her hands about as she talked. It was clear from her choice of words that the tremor in her voice was not caused by anxiety. I had found it fit to name her Crazy Feriha, somehow...

"It's like we have those kids on our own. By way of asexual reproduction... You men of the academic profession, who pick wives to suit your lives, are very keen to ignore this fact in every stage of the marriage. On the other hand, we have to give the mister his credit; at least he admitted that 'it suited him well.' There are many men who would not do that. Running the house, answering to all the needs of our husband and children, and returning to our jobs as soon as possible are all expected from us women."

The Initiator quickly jumped to his own defense and continued from where he had left off. "Like I was saying, I suggested finding a helper. It was the busiest time for me at work with my duties; so, she should have accepted this offer, since I wasn't there to help her and both of our parents lived far away from us. Well, we later found out why she was being so fastidious back then, but it was not something I could have recognized at that time. It never even crossed my mind."

Crazy Feriha was very quick to respond to him once again, "Your story is becoming mysterious."

"I wish it was mysterious; it's turning into a twilight series."

"Did your wife leave the kids with you and disappear? I know many people who think about doing that but are unable to."

"I couldn't say which way would be better now."

"And I don't know what else could be worse than that."

"I had a five-day conference in Japan, following a full week of arguments at home. Going that far away also meant being away from everything, so I was really looking forward to the trip. Lately, my wife has been in a very touchy mood. I was reluctant to go home, as she was always anxious and angry, would cry out of the blue, and in the middle of the daily chores, she would go out in the tiny summerhouse in the garden and sit there still until she was called in, and sometimes I'd have to call her a few times. It used to make me upset to think about going home. Knowing that in the place that was supposed to be my place of peace, a whole new challenge was waiting for me. After a full day of tackling other people's problems, I never wanted to go home. Hence, I began to accept the offers from my friends to go out for a drink after work as a chance to hide out."

"I am really sorry, but I see a road to twilight series for the poor lady here." Crazy Feriha could hardly control herself. She was moving up and down in her seat throughout this speech. I was waiting for her to explode. Other people at the table were following Feriha, not the Initiator. This meant that I was not the only one expecting the sky to fall from her end.

Finally, the Initiator showed signs of discomfort with these outbursts. With an even thicker voice, "Let me continue, Mrs. If you keep jumping in with your prejudiced conclusions, you may regret it in the end. That is, of course, assuming you are keen to avoid being unjust," he said.

I couldn't help thinking to myself, *Wow, wow, wow... How*

did this conversation become so sharp-edged and harsh?

It was surprising how people sat around the table were so unguarded and eager to share their most intimate memories, experiences, and thoughts. No one else except for the Initiator and Phillip knew each other before. This did not conform to the usual caution people who have just met display while they measure each other up. It was more like, "Well, we don't really know each other. Chances are we won't meet again after this gathering. So, I am going to tell the things I have carried inside for so long and say whatever crosses my mind without hesitation," way of thinking. Including me... I had a strong urge to spill out my most well-kept secrets. This was my chance to offload all my burdens before leaving this place.

Oscar Wilde was right when he once said, "Man is least himself when he talks in his own person. Give him a mask, and he will tell you the truth." The masks here were, perhaps, the fact that we would be seeing each other only this one time. Even though I had the urge to share my most guarded thoughts, I found what was being said very interesting. The teller was free of any fear of being criticized, judged, or excluded, which led to them sharing these events and their feelings, and especially their mistakes for all to see. The promise of telling the truth was the feeling of relief compared to the burden of keeping the lies.

Crazy Feriha bowed her head in acceptance of her mistake. In a very tainted voice, she said, "I am sorry. I guess we are all seeing through the window our own wounds have opened." Raising her voice slightly, she added, "Please continue. I am actually curious to hear how your story goes. If I am giving you the impression that I am only interested in my own, that's not my intention. Still, I may have overreacted since I have some sensitivity about this issue."

The fact that the Initiator continued to speak was a sign of his acceptance of Crazy Feriha's apology. At least that's what I thought.

"Japan is a long way away; the time difference and my lack of desire to contact home, the impact of the tense situation just before I left, were all reasons for me to see this five-day trip as an opportunity to be away from it all. However, on the way back, the realization of how much I had missed my wife and my daughters hit me. With the desire to get back to them soon and the feeling of guilt for being distant lately, I was determined to do anything to make up for this emptiness, for all our sakes. As I turned the key with excitement, the scene I faced inside was chilling."

We all understood that this was the scene from the horror movie that was mentioned earlier. As the Initiator brought his half-full glass of water to his lips, most likely to wet his dry throat, I realized that no one had touched their plates. The sauce, made up of a mixture of shredded, salted fish with finely chopped parsley, sat untouched on top of our penne. During this water break, as if it was pre-arranged, everyone took a bite of their pasta before resting their forks by the plates again. The Initiator—I should really call him the Father after all his revelations—continued as soon as he rested his glass on the table.

"All the furniture was packed in one corner. Our elder daughter was running around, the younger one's crying coming from the children's bedroom upstairs. My wife was cleaning the floor harshly with a cloth she had in her hand. I put my small suitcase on the floor and walked in without taking off my shoes. My wife turned my way, stared at my shoes, and continued to rub the floor, with a look of hatred still on her face. I didn't know what to do. I couldn't move for a while. Then I got the courage to go up to her. I knelt behind her. I held her shoulders with both hands and gently guided her up as I told her, 'Come on, honey, get up. We can clean it together later. You must be tired. Look, our baby is crying. Let's go see her together.' She tensed her shoulders. But then, shortly after, she relaxed and stood up. We went up to our baby's room; you may guess how I felt when I saw her exhausted of crying, perhaps even worst, of hunger and thirst—and of course how hard I had to try to keep this feeling from my wife."

"Please don't tell us that she didn't look after the baby while you were gone."

This outburst came from the young woman who'd been sitting silently next to Crazy Feriha up until this moment. She was almost screaming. I had also felt the same rebellion rising inside me. That was why, following this pretty woman, I had the courage to say, "How can such a thing happen? Oh my God, what happened to this woman's motherly instinct?" After having named the pretty woman as Barbie, I turned to her and said, "Good thing nothing disastrous happened to the kids. It would be impossible to live with that kind of regret." The Initiator, sorry, the Father, looked at each of us and calmly continued.

"I lost count of how many doctors I have taken her to. They were never able to diagnose it. I had to take care of both my wife and the children for days. All those busy times at work, well, I put it all aside. I had only one responsibility, and that was to keep us all alive. In the end, I called for my mother-in-law's help. I had to finally let her know of the situation, as the sleepless days and nights became unbearable. I had been trying to keep her from seeing her daughter and granddaughters in such a state, but I needed her help to prevent potentially a much worse consequence. My mother-in-law knew what was happening the moment she walked in. It appears that the elders were familiar with this condition. Right after that, it was a strange coincidence that the doctor we went to diagnosed her with postpartum depression—and possibly a psychosis-like condition."

"I had thought of that." Barbie was looking very proud of herself as she was saying this. The Father took a defensive stance.

"Oh really? Yet, neither I nor any of the other doctors we had seen could think of it. People generally find it hard to admit the facts when it comes to themselves or close relatives, and doctors' close family members are subject to this when getting medical aid. A famous sociologist defined this as 'expert's immunity.' In my opinion, this perfectly accounts for the situation I described here."

Just then, I started thinking about a mythological story I had learned about a year ago, *Alkarısı*. I had heard it from a gynecologist colleague of mine, during an unrelated conversation. He had told me that, in the past few years, women who recently gave birth would put on a blue or pink ribbon in their hair. He was angry that the traditional rituals were being changed without any consideration of their source and said, "The actual color is red. This tradition, which is centuries old, originates from the need to carry something red, as a way of avoiding a mythological monster called *Alkarısı*, who is believed to latch on to postpartum women to eat away their liver. Nowadays, it is adapted for the baby's gender; the ribbon is either blue or pink. To me, this is nonsense. I find it hard to accept. And then they talk behind my back like, 'the doctor is obsessed with the color of the ribbon.' I cannot keep quiet. What can I do?" According to this myth, ways to keep the monster away involved not leaving the woman alone, especially by a man staying with her, a red-colored dress, and placing a knife or a needle underneath her pillow. I was surprised to meet someone who had actually experienced what I had heard about at that time. This was a story from Anatolia. It was unlikely that the people around this table could have heard of it. However, as I knew that some stories were common in different cultures, I wondered if there was a similar monster in the Western spoken culture. To find out, I would have had to tell the *Alkarısı* myth in full length, and I didn't really feel like it. So, I shared a somewhat scientific fact, at least to demonstrate that I had some knowledge of the subject.

"Indeed, I am aware that after unwanted or illegitimate pregnancies, this condition can be observed when the mother is not ready for or afraid of giving birth. It is more commonly reported to be seen in women with a prior psychological disorder. I had also heard that, if it is not diagnosed early and treated in time, it may lead to suicide. You were lucky."

"Oh, tell me about it. They warned us about the risk of suicide. That's why I was always alert, not sleeping, or at most sleeping very lightly. I kept her under supervision. I didn't tell her mother about this risk. She would have been very alarmed. She mostly took care of the children. I mostly spied on my wife and took everything that could be dangerous out of her sight, and this took a lot of effort to do without her noticing. But it was worth it. We managed to get through the time it took for the medicines to work and eventually, everything was on track. When my wife thinks back on those times, she cannot believe that she was so far gone to have nearly harmed her own children. As for me, I am horrified to imagine what worse could have happened. Yes, it was me who wanted the second child the most, but she didn't object to it. It is impossible to know what thoughts or concerns lie in one's subconsciousness."

"Maybe, if the first birth was a difficult one, she may have been impacted by that," said Crazy Feriha.

"It was not difficult at all; in actual fact, it was an exceptionally easy one. We called the midwife when the contractions started. It was just five minutes after she had told us, 'Baby won't come that soon; time the intervals between contraction, and then call me and let me know.' My wife was suddenly screaming, her waters broke, and she lay down where she was. I had to assist my daughter's birth. Ten minutes after her first scream, the crying of my daughter was echoing in the kitchen. We called the midwife again, and she came right away and she handled the rest as I was wrapping up our baby warmly."

"In my opinion, this is a highly traumatic birth, all right. Who knows how she coded that in her brain?"

It was Barbie, making the final point. To me, this depressing subject had dragged on unnecessarily long. But, interestingly, the reason for those around the table coming together had turned into some kind of a "who's got the worst story" contest. I had the suspicion that, in the moment of silence, everyone was thinking, "There must be something worse I lived through that I could add some bells and whistles to and share, if I could, eh?"

A sudden silence fell on the crowd at the table. We ate a bit more of our penne. The service was very slow since there were a lot of us and this small mountain village restaurant was not used to having so many people. We found out that the main course was tuna fish, followed by our pasta as the starter. People at the large table in the middle had almost made it to their desserts while we were still waiting for the main course. We had all just about managed half of our plates, except the Silent Cowboy. He had polished his off. Perhaps, just as he was not talking much, he was also not a very keen listener. As the forks were placed at five o'clock on the round plates, a waiter came over and collected them. I really appreciate these kinds of subtle communications. Knowing what these mean and adopting them gives people a sense of belonging in a community of a certain culture. You'd have to spend some time with the people of that culture to know these nuances. I was pleasantly surprised when I found out why a glass of water was served with Turkish coffee, for instance. This apparently came about when it was considered rude for the host to ask the guests directly if they were hungry or not. The guest would drink the water first, to say "I am hungry" or the coffee first, to say, "I am not hungry." This way the host can place an extra plate on the table and kindly invite the guest to eat. Before I learned about leaving the fork and knife on at five o'clock on the plate, I had been to many restaurants and waited for a long while until I had to call the waiter to say, "You may take my plate."

Our silence continued for a while after each one of us had received our main courses. We all had learned our lesson; we had to eat it before it got cold, without talking. Besides, the fish was delicious. This time all the forks and knives were at five o'clock round about the same time. We leaned back. We looked at each other. We tried to see who was ready to say something. A couple of people said, "It was a delicious meal, right?" at the same time. Noises of approval came one after the other. And then there was another moment of silence… For some reason, I had a vision of the spotlights on a stage falling on me as I moved to the foreground. I felt my turn had come. I quietly cleared my throat. This resulted in all the faces turning to me; a voice inside me was rising, and the curtain…

"People get overwhelmed with the things they cannot tell. Secrets are a heavy burden, right?"

"Where did that statement come from, just like that?" It was

Barbie asking. She seemed truly surprised. And I was surprised that she was surprised. Wasn't this what everyone else who spoke had been doing? At least that's how I saw it. So I continued without an explanation. I was sure that Barbie, and all the others along with her, would be even more surprised as I carried on talking.

"What's worse is the lies... They are heavy like a metal armor. And as one lie leads to another, the liar sinks deeper into the swamp of despair."

I was determined. Tonight, I was going to get it over with, among this group of strangers who gathered at the table, who hadn't hesitated to share their most personal stories. The series of events that I was about to reveal had come to an end four years ago, having lasted for ten years. Although looking back on it now, I find it hard to make any kind of sense of it. It was me who had lived it all. Without a worry, believing its normal... I wanted to tell it.

"Considering how the evening progressed, I have something to tell as well. I will unload my heavy burdens. That is, if you would like to listen, of course."

"What kind of question is that? We are here to listen as long as you wish to tell. And you are probably right; it has turned into some kind of session where we unburden ourselves." The Father was the one giving me support. After all, he was the one to kick off the proceedings.

"I met him when I was in my second year of university. I was a bright student, a promising medical doctor candidate, according to my family and professors. This fact, which I internally rebelled against, was the very thing that led to my first conflicts as I emerged as a young adult from my obedient childhood. I should have known that since I couldn't openly express my feelings, they would find other ways to come out. I fell in love with my dance instructor the moment I first laid my eyes on him. He was twelve years older than me. We had taken an interest in Latin dances as a group of girls and we enquired at the first dance school that came our way. I don't remember how we all agreed it was a good idea, but we decided to start on that very day, and I was partnered with the instructor, Can. The excitement of him demonstrating every move with me and my instant crush merged together along the way; I was unable to tell these feelings apart. On top of it all, as he firmly grabbed me by my waist, I could feel the heat from his hands flowing into every cell of my body and turning into hot lava on my cheeks, which I could see from the mirror on the wall in front of us, and this made me burn even more. After the lesson, when we went out onto the street, comments from my friends about how lucky I was, and their jealousy-infused jokes, made me feel a little upset, but I was ready to take it all, just so we could continue the lessons."

Those at the table who spoke before me had all embellished their stories; they had kept the audience anticipating, whereas I had jumped straight in to tell the story in all its simplicity, perhaps only exaggerating my weaknesses unnecessarily. I wasn't going to be able to stay on the subject if I couldn't hold their attention. It was clear that people without a certain connection wouldn't feel the need to be polite to listen to the story to the end. If that were the case, I would miss this unique opportunity and have had to make way for the secrets of the next person waiting their turn to speak impatiently. I had better think of something striking to say to keep them wanting more. Yes, I had better, but how? It wasn't going to be easy, to turn it one hundred and eighty degrees around and tell what I had been conditioned to hide all these years as an interesting and colorful story. On the other hand, I could see that keeping this secret in me after this moment would be even harder.

"Let me say what I am supposed to say at the end right now. Because I don't want to cast a shadow on my story as I try to find a way to create a dense cloud of curiosity. By the way, although I have already announced that the killer is the servant, I hope to explain how the murder took place in an adequately interesting way."

I was devising a strategy of my own. I could only hope that it would work. My intention was just to tell it and get over with it. I mean, I wasn't after the best narrator prize. I was just tired of hiding that part of my life that harbored a massive lie. Especially, every time I met my mother would inevitably lead to a feeling of deep pain. I regretted the years I had stolen from her; I knew that I had to tell everything from the beginning to serve my sentence and be free, but could never find the courage. I couldn't bear to see the disappointment in her eyes when she found out. I couldn't do that to her, knowing that she always looked at me with a mixture of love and pride. I can't imagine it would be easy to face the truth when you find out that your daughter, who'd been the sole meaning of your life, had been lying to you for such a long time, and such a big lie too?

"Until four years ago from now, I had been a ghost bride for ten years. I lived a life that only my boyfriend, his parents, and a few of his closest relatives knew about. Since my family was living in a different city and their business didn't allow them to come and visit me often, I was able to hide it from them. And ever since I left it all behind, I've been living in remorse. All my conversations with Mom end up with the vision of me screaming out that I am not worthy of her love and trust in my head. But I cannot do this in reality. I worry that she may never trust me again. That chapter of my life is over and I am now married, legally, to someone my family approves of, and in fact, really loves. It felt so natural back then when I was living that lie; now it embarrasses me. My only consolation is that my husband accepts and loves me as I am, despite knowing about it all. I have never even thought of hiding this from him; I not only told him the whole truth about my past, but also made a promise that I would never have to lie to anyone, including him. Earlier, when I was talking about the burden of secrets and being crushed under the heavy load of lies, this is what I meant. You would have to live it to truly know it."

I examined each face. I was trying to see the impact of what I was saying had on them. None of them gave it away. It wasn't that they were not interested, but they didn't seem judgmental either. Could they see themselves in my position? I couldn't tell from their faces.

Barbie spoke, "Even if your parents were in another city, you are talking about a period of ten years; how could they not realize it, and not even suspect anything?"

"I told them I was renting a house with a school friend. In actual fact, I was living with Can and his parents. His mother loved me like I was her own child. To tell you the truth, it was more heartbreaking knowing that I wasn't going to see her again than breaking up with Can. What I had with Can consumed us both, and in the end, love had burned out. But I got closer to his mother as we shared more and more. Can and I decided that we had to keep our relationship with others. The reason for this was the age gap and our different social backgrounds. These were both considered unacceptable in our society and we wanted to preserve our love rather than fighting against the norm. So, we chose the easy path; hiding."

As I paused for breath, I hoped that my audience would have a moment to contemplate their own experiences of social exclusion. Then I continued my story before I lost their attention completely.

"I had actually tried to open up to my parents at the very beginning. I had never done anything without them knowing until then. My mother's reaction was most unusual; she almost went crazy. I had only mentioned that I had a crush on my dance instructor, who was a couple of years older than me. 'Never!' she said, 'I could never stand back and watch you destroy your life.' I was deeply in love; I simply could not comprehend and accept how she would see this as me destroying my life. When I mentioned what had happened to Can, he said, 'Don't worry, they don't need to know.' This sounded sensible. So I went to my mom and said, 'Fine, have it your way; I will never see him again.' The following week, I moved in with Can and his family. We started living in secret, fearing that my parents might find out. For example, while I was a student, we couldn't go on holiday together, because I had to spend my holidays with my parents. When I started working, we managed a few short getaways. Many of these trips would end with us fighting and the moments I thought were my happiest would soon turn sour. Yet, we had an unexplainable bond that masked these unpleasant times, perhaps like a curtain hides the darkness at night. So many things I wasn't aware were lacking back then now seem absurdly unacceptable. We don't have a single photograph of us, for instance. We would only take pictures of each other. This used to make me think that we didn't really have a shared history. If I complained about it, Can calmly look into my eyes and say that we were breaking the mold with our unusual relationship. And I would believe him."

At this stage of my story, Phillip didn't neglect to add the male point of view. "Instead of trying to change things, he made them easier to accept. Despite such secrets being hard to keep, he must have thought that it would still require less effort than standing up to your family and social prejudices."

Crazy Feriha answered Phillip before I had a chance, "As women, we tend to have a more emotional approach rather than be concerned with saving effort. Our relationships are influenced by our interactions with close family and friends. The time we spend with them strengthens our bond as a couple."

"But then, when the love is gone, both sides feel trapped. Things they once enjoyed sharing with each other turn into things they have to bear." This counterargument came from Phillip, of course. I continued regardless, keeping my turn as I broke up the banter between the two of them.

"Can's mother really wanted to come to my graduation, and I really wanted her to be there. But this was not possible. Because both of my parents had put their work aside for this and even took my sister out of school to attend. That evening, we went out for dinner as a family. Right after I left them at the airport, I ran straight back to my secret family for another celebration with them. Can and I had made a choice, and knowing that this had some consequences for the ones we loved, even at degrees that they may never know, fills me with regret. Back then, I was content with the belief that I was going with the flow and doing what was necessary to move on with my life."

Since the discussion was around lies and lying, Crazy Feriha thought that a true punishment for a liar would not only be that others don't believe him, but that he loses the ability to trust others himself. Following this, we all sat silently for a moment, and I am fairly certain that everyone else was contemplating this just like I was. As someone regarded as honest by others, and having hated lies in principle, I carry that time of my life as a stain on my soul. Knowing how I lived through this, believing it was OK now, makes me reluctant to trust others. Is this some kind of punishment? Yes, it is; this is a punishment for not building my relationships on trust...

The Father spoke for the first time since he had his turn with his story at the start. I thought that he wasn't listening, but perhaps having a hard time reliving his own story after telling it. I was wrong. We found out that he also had a similar experience before he got married. When they were dating his current wife, her family was against them getting married. They offered no specific reason for it either. They were just against it. The Father was very offended by this as he had thought that he would be considered an ideal husband by many. Trusting in the strength of their love, they continued seeing each other in secret for about a year. One lie led to another. The situation got a little tricky when his girlfriend got pregnant. With their juvenile and inexperienced ways, they tried to find a solution to this. But it was not easy since they were broke as students. The Father borrowed some money from his parents, saying that it was to help a friend in need. They didn't know what to do or where to go, but they found a way somehow. They managed to have an abortion. However, Annie—his lover then and wife now—could never get over this loss. She couldn't forgive herself. She went through a major depression. She stopped eating and drinking; she started to cut off all her ties with life as she hid behind her veil of pain. Since her parents knew nothing about what was going on, they put her depression down to their forced break up. Concerned about her mental and physical health, they gave them their blessing for marriage. It wasn't easy for the Father to get her to start a new life and leave the unbearable loss they lived through behind. His perseverance finally paid off, and she came out of depression. They made an unspoken pact to never mention what had happened. When the Father was done telling this, he concluded, "So I have personally lived and seen for myself that lies lead to more lies and terrible consequences." And then he fell back into silence.

I was taken aback by what he said about the unwanted pregnancy and the way it was ended. So much so that I was ready to make another confession. I almost did, but just as I was about to say, "me too..." I stopped. A voice inside me warned me, *That's too far!* I wasn't going to tell the rest of the story. So, I said, "Since I had also seen for myself that one lie leads to another, I put an end to this nonsensical life," and ended my speech, hoping to change the topic.

Crazy Feriha turned to the Father and said that what his wife lived through after giving birth to their second child could be related to what he had just told us. The Father bowed his head. It wasn't clear if he was evaluating this statement in his head or agreeing with it.

As if to tell us to wrap up the conversation with a sweet taste, our desserts arrived. Everyone looked really tense. Our battered souls were so full of emotions that none of us could handle it any more. We all needed a moment to settle.

We had made it to the end of dinner—our session. As we had our espressos, we talked about how the day went, discussed the proceedings of the meeting, recalled a few funny moments, and laughed. I was the first to leave. I wished everyone a good night. "Tomorrow will be another long and busy day." I left the restaurant and started walking back to my hotel through the same narrow streets. There was no fog that night. I realized why when

I turned into one of the streets leading to the sea. A sudden strong wind chilled me to the bone. I shivered. It felt like the continuation of the chill I felt not long ago when I told my story. I lifted the collars of my coat and wrapped my scarf up around my neck and mouth. I put my hands in my pockets.

I was desperate to get warm. I often feel the cold more when I am in such mood. I was literally shaking when I arrived in my room. I jumped into the bed with my clothes on. It was not enough; so I threw over the extra blanket. I knew that I'd be all right if I could go to sleep. I closed my eyes. But I was not able to sleep. If I could pull myself together, just enough so I could perform my bedtime rituals, but I couldn't.

I was abroad, far away from home, in a village on top of a mountain. As if that wasn't enough, there was the feeling of isolation caused by being on an island. The things I had heard and told at the table had awakened many conflicting feelings within me. The hotel was converted from a very old monastery. With its high ceilings, wooden windowsills, wooden shutters, and simple décor, it had a feel of a retreat. This suited me well, as I felt I needed to be alone. Alongside the guilt, I could feel anger rising inside me for not being able to forgive myself. I had hoped that I would feel some sort of relief for pouring my heart out in front of the others, but instead, I had lost my self-respect.

As I tossed and turned in bed with depressing thoughts, I couldn't help but notice the whirling of the wind. It was coming in through the windows, under the door, any crack it could find, and leaving some other way as quickly as it arrived. It appeared that a big storm had hit outside. It sounded like rain was pouring down too. And it was not going to stop anytime soon. I remembered I had not brought an umbrella with me, sadly. Although I had brought several warm clothes, it looked like I'd have to wear a few jumpers all at once. Taking the rain into account, though, these clothes weren't going to keep me dry. There was no point in trying to go to the meeting in this weather. Even if I could walk in this storm, getting wet in the rain would only risk becoming ill. I was so anxious I became short of breath. When I finally accepted that I wasn't going to fall asleep, I forced myself out of bed. I wrapped myself in a blanket. As I made my way to the bathroom, I stopped by the black shutter to listen to the sound of the wild wind and nervously opened one side ajar. Oh... There was no rain. What I heard must have been the leaves churning. The wind hadn't gotten stronger since I got back to my room at all. As for the storm? No sign of it... I was relieved.

I was beginning to see that certain signs, or maybe even answers without questions, had been placed in different parts of life. For me, these signs were saying, "Don't fret about your woes unnecessarily, just open the window and look, face the truth. In most cases, truth is not what you fear it to be." I opened my bag and took a *frutta Martonara* from the paper bag. I put it whole in my mouth; as its taste filled my mouth, I was filling up with content. I wanted more, so I took another one. Now I was ready to brush my teeth. In the bathroom, I looked in the mirror. I saw myself smile back at me. I nodded as if to say thank you. The other me nodded in response, cracking a smile.

Suddenly, it was all very clear in my head. *The meeting will end tomorrow. I'll head back home. I'll go to see my mother straight away. I'll sit in front of her and tell her everything, the entire truth. Tell her all the things I now consider being a mistake and the lessons I have learned. I can try to explain my reasons for keeping these from her and ask for forgiveness.*

Knowing that my confessions would potentially cause her a great deal of disappointment, I was ready to face the consequences. I had no doubt that she loved me, so I thought I could regain her trust and I was ready to do whatever it would take. With these thoughts, I felt warmer. As I put on my pajamas, I returned to normality.

With these mood swings, I felt the weariness settle on me. I lay down in my rather small bed, with one blanket on me. I imagined myself walking toward the sea with my hair blowing in the wind, which was turning into a sweet melody.

Lace Baskets

For seven years, Azize had been looking after her husband, who had been bedridden; with love and care. The parental role they had postponed in the haste of youth and then chose to forget by saying that the time had passed had become the essence of all her roles during this time. Moreover, she was playing this role with all her heart. However, even those who lived through it could acknowledge it, and even those who hadn't, would admit saying, "It's really tough, honestly," to tackle the demanding endeavor.

Throughout this period, she had two male assistants by her side. This choice had seemed strange to those who didn't know her. Among those who knew her, some thought that her choice was inconvenient, but they had refrained from telling Azize about it because they knew it wouldn't make a difference. Those closest to her, with her when she made this decision, already knew the reasons. By thinking out loud, Azize said, "In the beginning, it might be fine, but as time goes on and Fahir's movements decrease, lifting and carrying him would require muscle strength, and putting him on a wheelchair would demand the same." This decision was a result of Azize's organized, forward-thinking, action-oriented nature throughout her entire life. The later objections came from those who said she had overlooked getting help for household chores. However, without feeling the need to explain at length, she contented herself with nodding slowly, as if she knew something they didn't.

In fact, Azize's mind was very clear about her decision. She had known Sabri for years, since he was a young man. When he had applied to the company she worked at, the softness of his gaze and the determination in his expression about what he expected had caught Azize's attention. Although the manager had opposed by saying that Sabri did not possess the required qualities, Azize had firmly stated without any room for objection that she would personally nurture this young man and eventually he could attend to all their needs. It was a demanding request, even harder to fulfill promise; because the person to be hired had to perform not only cleaning and cooking but also ironing. Aside from the obligation for all employees to wear the same uniform, ironing these uniforms to perfection was an uncompromisable condition in the workplace. It wasn't necessary to be a fortune teller to realize that Sabri, a young man who had come from the village, wouldn't be able to perform any of these tasks up to the expected standards. But Azize possessed a unique ability that came to the rescue in such times—an intuition to see hidden talents in the people she encountered and to bring forth those skills even before the individuals themselves were aware of them.

 Sabri quickly elevated his cleaning skills to a remarkable level and became a master of cooking, presenting feasts to the taste buds, and he became unrivaled in ironing. Azize took pride in her accomplishments. However, during the process, she hadn't spared Sabri from gentle reprimands and had gone to great lengths to explain everything meticulously, sometimes almost tearing her hair out in frustration. Nevertheless, she didn't give up; she had held Sabri's hand, repeatedly ironed the same white cotton pants, polished not only the sinks but also the kitchen counters, and made him buy the ingredients for crème caramel again and recreated it from scratch. The efforts from that time found their place many years later when they took care of Fahir together for the past seven years. Sabri never fell behind; Azize had known for a very long time that he could handle every task without needing anyone's help. Because she never entrusted the cooking to anyone, she didn't allow Sabri to prepare meals at home.

All other household chores and supporting Fahir's care were Sabri's responsibilities. The janitor of the adjacent building, Bilal, had also caught Azize's attention with his precision in shopping tasks. Bilal was also very skilled in interpersonal relationships. For over a decade, the janitor of their building had been changing frequently, but Azize only entrusted Bilal with the household's needs. These two men, one taking care of external tasks and the other handling household affairs, made Azize's life easier. Although Fahir rarely left the house, Azize, who preferred to keep her mind at home, was able to maintain a life where she was always at the center of everything. This woman, who cherished her freedom, managed to be everywhere without any impediment, even the limitations of her advanced age.

***

It was seven years ago. After spending long years placing their work at the center of their shared lives, courtesy of their solidarity in being from the same profession, Azize and Fahir's life routines changed in the year they retired. Just like any other day, Azize went to bed early, and Fahir had mentioned that he would write something before going to sleep. Fahir's biggest dream for his retirement was to write a book. For this purpose, he had been trying to write every night until his pen ran dry for a few years now. Reading it to Azize in the morning and getting her opinion was a unique excitement. Like his other dreams, this one wouldn't make sense without Azize's involvement.

That morning, Fahir woke up but couldn't get out of bed. When he got over the initial shock, he realized he had no strength on his right side. Azize had already gotten up and was doing her morning exercises, which she never avoided. Although Fahir could hear faint noises from the living room, he couldn't call out for help. He didn't yet know if this voice loss was reversible. He would have to wait for Azize to return to the bedroom to take a shower and change. Although Fahir tried to remain calm, as the minutes went by, he began to get anxious. He couldn't predict what health issue lay ahead for them or what difficulties they would encounter while trying to solve it. Forty years together is not a short time... He had always looked after his wife and devoted his life to ensuring she never experienced the slightest discomfort. What wouldn't he do to find a way to keep Azize away from all this? Of course, it wasn't even an option to do this against Azize's wishes.

Azize also panicked when she recognized that Fahir might have a serious health problem. They rushed to the hospital; after tests and consultations with doctors, the diagnosis they already knew was confirmed; stroke. Due to a few clots blocking his brain vessels, weakness had appeared in Fahir's right arm and leg, and damage had occurred in his speech center. Sometimes, although rarely, these strokes could be partial and temporary. The necessary treatment had begun, and the rest was left to the body's ability to recover and, to a large extent, luck. Only time would show how Fahir's illness would progress. The problem that hindered his speech had been quickly resolved.

However, time chose not to be impartial regarding his movement limitations. Fahir lived for five years, neither improving nor deteriorating in this physical condition. He rarely left the house, but he followed the physiotherapist's recommendations meticulously at home, with the help of Sabri and Azize. Even on weekends, the therapists followed the instructions on what exercises to perform at home. At Azize's request, Sabri and Bilal installed metal handrails on all the walls of the house and created a walking path. They were all fighting against impaired mobility, putting in great effort. Although it was difficult to maintain hope, imagining that Fahir would fully recover someday gave them strength. Moreover, Azize had always enjoyed taking care of patients and looking after them with compassion. When it came to Fahir, he was her precious to look after with love.

The two years following the first five years were downhill. The burden of illness was compounded by old age. Fahir's physical strength had decreased significantly compared to his past vigor. Nevertheless, he used to say to Azize, "There's nothing left in my mind. Taking a breath beside you is a grace for me." Azize knew the profound meaning of this statement very well.

When he lost the desire to get out of bed, they slowly began discussing how the end would come. Fahir would initiate the topic, and Azize would force herself to speak with the same composure. Fahir didn't want to go into intensive care. Having spent his life in hospitals, he had pondered over this matter on many occasions. Back then, he stood by every word he said, especially those meant for other patients or their relatives. From his perspective, being the subject of the matter was the only difference now. He believed that people had the right to leave this world in their homes, by the side of their loved ones. Just as he held his beloved mother's finger with the most basic reflex when he came into this world, he wanted to hold the hand of his most beloved woman, his dear wife, when he left, and take his final breath while looking into those deep oceanic eyes.

He didn't need to persuade Azize. After spending a long and intense lifetime together, they had learned to understand each other without words, not through passive acceptance, but through a unity of heart and mind. Yet people wouldn't remain silent. To those who questioned how she could do this, Azize would reply, "I will respect his will of steel, as always." She couldn't bear the thought of being even a moment apart from her life companion or learning that everything had ended like ordinary news from a stranger. Moreover, for her to spend the rest of her life in tranquility, they needed to pass over their shared memories with various emotions one last time, to be on the lookout for the moment she would say the final words she reserved for the very last moment, and to leave no room for regrets. Their sweet guest joined to their life just around these days.

***

Canan was a young woman in her thirties. Her mother was an old friend of Azize since secondary school. Years later, Fahir had helped her during Canan's birth. Normal births were his responsibility, while C-sections were Azize's job. They had divided the work from the very beginning like this, because that's what Azize wanted. In the times when there were no opportunities for women doctors to perform surgeries, they embarked on their careers, and Fahir, who had witnessed Azize's surgical passion throughout her training, had unconditionally accepted her preferences. Moreover, he had always watched Azize in admiration without needing to say a word.

Beyond being an obstetrician, Azize was a physician with a

holistic view. She was passionate about her profession. Describing her would mean describing her profession; it was not an optional but a necessary choice. Her personality, her eyes, her hair, her childhood, and her old age were secondary to her because that's what she wanted to be recognized. The qualities that could describe her way of life best were her medical profession and her freedom.

When they went to a mountain village for a summer vacation with her sister and her sister's husband during their youth, they had cleaned up an abandoned old health center with the village women and had received the support of the village imam for this, and they had taken care of patients there throughout the vacation. Luckily, her sister, İmer, was also crazy enough to agree with her on such projects.

When they found a speculum waiting unused in the health center's storage room in the town nearby that they had walked to, she rejoiced as if she had found a treasure. She had to make a considerable effort; she persisted and spoke, to borrow it despite it not being used. She had cleaned it thoroughly, soaked it in disinfectant liquid, and started using it for examining women. She had never mentioned this memory to anyone on their holiday return and had stored it in her unvalued memories archive to talk about it if she found someone who would appreciate it. Also, nobody knew that she was the one performing C-sections.

In the outside world, where they appeared as a doctor couple entering surgeries together when it came time to perform the surgery, the transfer of the scalpel from Fahir to Azize occurred smoothly and naturally. However, because normal births required patience, it wasn't suitable for Azize, who was always impatient, to wait for a long time; therefore, it was inevitable that these tasks fell to Fahir in their division of labor.

Canan, when she was born into Fahir's hands, was very weak. Therefore, Azize and Fahir didn't leave alone the mother having her second child at a late age since Canan needed to be kept in the incubator and closely monitored. After seeing that Canan held onto life tightly in a short period, they left the mother and daughter behind with peace of mind. Everyone was busy with their own concerns. However, they went to Canan's first birthday party. Then, many years passed, one after the other.

When Canan got into medical school, she found them by chance. They talked on the phone. Despite being in the same city, they couldn't manage to meet up. But Canan preserved this loose bond between them by calling them on many special occasions. Years later, one day, when Canan called Fahir to invite him to her graduation ceremony, they wanted to attend, and went to the indoor sports hall where the ceremony would be held. Even though they couldn't find Canan and her family in the crowd, they had seen her from a distance when she went on stage. They waved at her, and they even threw the red carnations they had in their hands from the stands toward the stage.

Later, when they talked about this scene on the phone, they laughed a lot and had fun speculating about the fate of the bouquet of flowers. They communicated sporadically from Canan's compulsory duty place. Canan started her specialization training again in another city. Life's hustle and bustle had demanded their attention again, and their phone calls had been cut off—until six months ago...

One afternoon, Canan reached out to them from their unchanged home phone number. Azize answered the phone. Canan was going to ask Fahir if he could be her wedding witness. Since they were in the same city at last, she could come and see them. Azize didn't know how to tell Canan about Fahir's health condition; she could only say, "Come, my dear, you can ask him yourself." They arranged a time for the visit.

Azize opened the door in a very stylish robe. It was around noon. She looked quite fresh. She was wearing a white robe covered with blue and pink enamel flowers, matching her white velvet slippers with blue pom-poms. Although Canan was surprised at first, she remembered that it had been fashionable to wear a robe in the house. Because getting dressed and leaving the house required careful preparation, instead of putting on something right after getting out of bed, women carried the robe elegance to breakfast and the subsequent morning coffee sessions. She must have had a few robes given by her mother too, but she hadn't been able to create a suitable environment for this habit at any point in her life, so who knows where she left them? Canan came to herself with the anxiety that her thoughts would be understood. "Hello, I'm Canan. We finally managed to get together for real. How interesting. You look just like I imagined in my mind."

Azize responded with a smile, "Welcome, Canan. I felt the same way. Would you believe it? You did good to come."

Azize felt the need to explain, comparing her own appearance with Canan's stylish one and thinking she noticed her puzzlement from her gaze. "I've gotten used to wearing robes; I didn't think to change when I thought of your arrival. These have been waiting in the closet for years. Even though I bought them with care, I never got to use them. Retirement served this purpose too. When we were working in our own job, we delayed our retirement decision quite a bit, and finally, spending time at home ceased being a dream. Now I wear all sorts of them, and I enjoy it."

While they were talking, they had moved to the living room.

Canan's eyes looked for Fahir. Instead of him, Sabri came from inside. He sincerely said, "Welcome" to the young girl he met for the first time. He looked at the host. After Azize nodded, Sabri turned and walked away in the corridor. Canan hadn't understood what was happening, but a little later, when she saw Sabri bringing Fahir in a wheelchair toward the living room, she froze. Azize and Canan made eye contact. They silently agreed to discuss the details later. Canan turned fondly toward Fahir, stopped the wheelchair at the door, and reached out his hands. Fahir weakly shook Canan's hand with his left hand and seemed to feel Canan with his weak right hand. He whispered softly, "You did good to come." A few ordinary sentences that didn't go beyond inquiring about each other's well-being were exchanged. Afterward, Canan didn't know what to say, and Fahir remained silent due to his lack of strength. While Sabri pushed the wheelchair back to the bedroom, Canan stared after them. Right at that moment, Azize took Canan's arm and told her that Fahir shouldn't get tired. Guiding Canan, she led her toward the long sofa by the window in the dining room. After pointing for her to sit there, she took her usual seat in the armchair across from her.

The half-drunk water with lemon slices in the crystal glass on the side table and the folded newspaper suitable for reading on it indicated that Azize spent most of her time in that chair. There was so much to talk about, and oh, how difficult it was. Canan explained that the wedding invitation was partly a cover for her visit and that there was actually no set date for the wedding yet. They didn't continue the subject. Instead, with the guidance of this introduction, the conversation soon shifted to how Azize and Fahir had met and married. Since both didn't feel ready to talk about the health issues that had affected Fahir, they were saved by pleasant memories. Moreover, Azize, with her deep intuition, had decided that love stories would be good for Canan.

According to what Azize said, she had started her specialization two years after Fahir. She was twenty-six, and Fahir was twenty-eight years old. Both were assistant doctors in the same department of gynecology and obstetrics. Fahir, as a senior doctor, helped Azize with daily hospital work, just like he did for other assistants. Seeing Fahir by her side during the most difficult times was a great source of comfort.

At the same time, she couldn't help but wonder how he was perceiving, how he was keeping up. They had become a crowded group of assistants. Despite being individuals with different interests, they managed to work collaboratively within the division of labor, a moderate hierarchy, and even outside the hospital, they spent time together in small groups. The proximity of interests determined who would be together.

Criteria like those who loved cinema, those who went to the theater at least once a month, those who enjoyed meetings where books were discussed, and those who preferred quiet environments like homes for evening get-togethers instead of music-filled places were all applicable to both. Moreover, Fahir would give Azize the books he had finished reading, and he wouldn't take them back without discussing them with her. Their tastes had gradually converged. Even the things they didn't like were similar.

A few times, they had united against unfairness done to their friends and stood up together, and a few times, they had conveyed their joint suggestions to the head of the department through Fahir for better functioning. Whatever was going wrong immediately caught their attention, and they would run to tell each other and start looking for solutions. Their friendship mostly happened within the group, growing slowly but steadily.

One day, Azize fell seriously ill. Since she had never displayed any delicate or fragile behaviors before, the entire team became anxious. Because of her diligence, eagerness to learn, and skillfulness, she was the apple of her professor's eyes. Being always ready to help and having a caring and strong friendship had earned her the affection of her colleagues. Azize's health was getting worse. The professors intervened and arranged for her to have a private room in the hospital, ensuring her comfort and the best care possible.

Friends at work took turns spending time with her; in a way, they had established a rotation system to accompany her. Especially Fahir, every morning, would bring his battery-powered radio to Azize's side as soon as he arrived at the hospital, and in the evening, he would take the radio and go home. At night, the girls took turns staying by Azize's side. They made sure she rested and slept without tiring her too much. The busyness of the day didn't allow for her friends to visit, and since Azize always liked having people around, the radio was perfect to carry voices, words, and melodies to her. Being away from work was a good consolation. And then, there were books…

All her friends, but especially Fahir, brought books and magazines to her hospital room. And he carried frequently the almond cookies… He would buy them fresh out of the oven, inhaling their delicious smell as he brought them through the hospital corridors without sealing the bag, capturing that aroma. The first bite of the soft cookie was the best remedy for the metallic taste of the medication left in the mouth. When Azize ate more than three in a row, Fahir's medical side would emerge, and he would sweetly restrain her, saying, "Young Lady, excess of everything is harmful for you these days." Yet, since he couldn't resist, he would leave the bag within Azize's reach, trusting that Azize would heed his warning and he would go about his duties.

One evening, when Fahir came to get the radio, he suddenly said to Azize, "I love you."

Azize looked at his warm smile and replied, "I love you too, Fahir!" Fahir's heart would have skipped a beat out of joy, but the continuation of the sentence followed, "Don't people love their friends?"

Fahir remained silent for a while, contemplating whether to continue speaking. *Was silence or speech riskier in terms of losing something?* He would have given anything to know the answer to this question. The arrow had already been released from the bow. How many sleepless nights could he endure before missing this opportunity?

"I... I love you, not just as a friend, I mean, more than a friend, Azize! Know that I will love you for a lifetime."

Azize, unexpectedly faced with this confession, was tongue-tied. Although she tried to weigh her words, the pounding of her heart, sweaty palms, and the icy sweat running down her back prevented her from doing so. The principle of telling the truth, regardless of the outcome, conflicted with the risk of losing a friend like Fahir, and she couldn't predict which one would prevail. Nevertheless, she knew she had to give an answer, and her anxiety was increasing. Meanwhile, Fahir tried to stop the ebb and flow he noticed with Azize by saying, "You don't have to give an answer now. Just say you'll think about it."

It wasn't like Azize to do this; she should have clarified her feelings right there and then. She quickly put an end to the delay, which she had offered ambivalently, due to her rush, "I've never felt in that way about you, Fahir, you've always been my best friend." Azize had stopped suddenly at that part of the telling. As she continued narrating, the same mist that had appeared in Azize's eyes that day settled in again. *When Fahir heard these words, his face aged a thousand years. He rose slowly from the chair, stood for a few seconds, and with a simple 'I understand' he turned his back and walked toward the door. He was wearing a black cashmere coat. His broad shoulders seemed to sag under the weight of the coat. The big man seemed to have become tiny. He quickly walked away with large strides. As the door closed, I could finally gather myself. First, I said to myself, what have I done? How could I do this? Then I leaned back and forth with various thoughts. The sleep in the hospital room wasn't really sleep, but that night, it turned into a nightmare with my eyes open. I wished for morning to come quickly. I was afraid I might go crazy if he didn't come to me. However, he came in at the same time with his radio in his hand. Although he had returned to his usual self, his voice was a thousand years old; his soul, too. I told him that I had been eagerly waiting for him and said, 'I love you too, Fahir. I accept your marriage proposal.' We were young again, young and strong, friends and lovers, hopeful for the future and ready to be each other's.*

Canan felt that what she heard from Azize were not just memories, but rather like lanterns that illuminated her path. Various emotions were awakened within her, and she sensed that she would find answers to some of her questions and sometimes even to the questions she hadn't even thought to ask. Holding her breath, she closed herself off from the world, opening up only to Azize as she listened to her. It was as if she was drinking from a spring that she rested her lips on during the hottest days. She was either realizing her thirst anew or there was a cry for help, not yet able to surface, that suddenly drew her here. The eye of the heart must surely open hastily. Since that day, she had been visiting that house at least every other day. Always at the same time, but with different moods. However, the moment she entered, she was filled with the joy of living. Contrary to her expectations of melancholy and worry dominating the house, she would leave behind her sorrows every time, reconnect with life, and perceive love, devotion, and persistence in a different light than before. Simultaneously, she questioned her own life and choices. For everything that upset her or troubled her, the question *"Could I be in a worse situation than them, really?"* gnawed at her. Since both the yes and no answers to the question would cause her pain, she chose to ignore it.

Canan could never get enough of listening to Azize. When Azize spoke, she maintained unbroken eye contact with the person in front of her, making her stories, regardless of their content, into an eye-to-eye conversation. Whether it was a recipe, the mischievous acts of the children she encountered while walking to the park during her short lunch breaks, the current state of her health problems, or her childhood memories, she spoke with the same enthusiasm. It fascinated Canan to see that she valued both the listener and what was being said. She especially loved how Azize approached every aspect of life with the same childlike wonder. Azize was an excellent speaker. She skillfully constructed her sentences, placing subjects, objects, and predicates in their proper places, without succumbing to the natural languor of spoken language. Moreover, she infused her sentences with the appropriate emotions, adding them to just the right dosage. And these emotions were contagious. Canan knew that these meetings, crowned by a delightful conversation that made time disappear, would lead her to say, "If she talks, I'll listen; if she tells, I'll understand!" She felt a kind of addiction to these conversations, and after they ended, the way back home seemed shorter as she tried to process her various emotions.

On another one of these meeting days, the conversation flowed and meandered until it grew and expanded, eventually reaching Azize's childhood and early youth in Heybeliada. Her azure eyes began to shine more vividly as she spoke. She talked about her father, Eczacı Yusuf, who was the most handsome and the most unpredictable man on the island, and her beautiful mother, Müdrike. Their marriage had barely lasted until the year her twin sister and she turned seven. Her father, captivated by the love of one woman, her mother, and ready to move on to another woman's love, had left their home. Azize had chased after him, calling out to him as he left, but her mother had to quickly shut the door. As Azize pleaded with her mother to open the door, her sister, İmer had yelled, "Understand it already. Dad doesn't want us!"

Azize's voice broke as she spoke about this event for the first time to Canan. She paused here, quietly trying to regain her composure. Then she continued. This time, her voice was calmer; the tone had lightened, as if the weight she had been carrying had been finally lifted, with the effect of releasing something she had kept hidden for a long time.

Once she began, the rest followed. The twin sisters had buried this pain deep beneath a thick veil and never talked about it again. But on days when guests came over, they would play outside the wooden door of the living room that was always closed and listen to their maternal grandmother complaining to the neighbors. They would escape to the garden to avoid hearing these conversations. On her first-grade report card, there was her father's signature, but her mother had signed the second and subsequent ones. They hadn't seen their father until they reached high school.

During those years they spent at their grandfather's house in Heybeliada, Azize didn't remember any image of a father or longing for him. Although she was surprised by this later, she thought it was a shared defense mechanism they had developed without discussing it, an unspoken understanding. During those days and afterward, the remedy for their soul's chill had been the warm love of their maternal grandmother.

Because back then, especially on the island, being the first woman to get divorced, giving up her high school education for the sake of her first love, and trying to cope with this disappointment along with the shame had turned her mother's balance upside down. The gentle-mannered mother had been replaced by a woman who yelled and slapped often. Their grandfather was angry about this and would tap his daughter's back firmly if he witnessed it. At that moment, the twin siblings would try to protect their mother, saying, as an excuse for the bite, "Grandpa, she didn't hurt us either; look, she even made a watch on my wrist!"

When their mother finally found herself again, they were embraced with love once more, but the wound from their early years had turned into a thick shell instead of healing entirely. This shell had the power to transform small blows into disproportionately large pains whenever they happened to hit.

Azize and İmer have become the sweethearts of the entire island as conjoined twins. Their maternal grandmother, who had fled from Thessaloniki to Heybeliada during the Balkan War, came as a new bride. Leaving behind their house, fields, and lands, she put enough gold in the large pocket of her kitchen apron and came to Turkey, leaving behind their past and maybe even their future. They were settled on Heybeliada with the other immigrants of that time. Due to their grandfather's good education, he became the postmaster of the island. They lived in the apartment above the post office. In those times of scarcity, their grandmother's resourcefulness in making things happen, her willingness to do so for anyone who asked, and her ability to gain the admiration of the native women had made her well-liked. Münevver Hanım, their grandmother, sewed clothes not only for themselves but also for others, not for money, but out of love to help their neighbors. The women generally paid for everything they received from each other with what they produced themselves. This trade tradition had become established among the neighbors by virtue of their grandmother.

One day, as payment for a wedding dress she had sewn, Münevver Hanım received two rolls of fabric; one dark blue, the other white. Despite never sewing clothes from blue and white fabric due to the influence of the past, she couldn't resist the insistence of Azize and İmer. The twins, who were thirteen years old at the time, convinced their grandmother not only to use the fabrics they fell in love with at first sight but also to sew a dress according to their collective design. Their grandmother quickly sewed two dresses with the fabrics, both full-buttoned dresses with narrow waists; one white and the other blue. The dresses were designed in a way that the buttons on the skirt and the top two buttons would open when they left the house and close when they returned, creating a visible and hidden effect, resembling a modern *bindallı*, a traditional folkloric caftan with the partite long skirt, in the blue dress with white shorts, and vice versa. The fun came to an end when they were caught by their grandfather as they were coming from the opposite direction, while their skirts were fluttering like flags. Those dresses never came out of the wooden chest again, and the topic was forgotten.

Azize saw that what she was saying had caused a pause in Canan's mood, so she continued. On the other hand, happy days in a group of friends, both boys and girls, continued without a hitch; happy days, boat rides, and sibling-like friendships. After sharing these memories, Azize thought for a while, as if lost in thought, reliving those lively days on the island. Then she looked at Canan and said, "I'm telling you this so that you know; these things were happening in this country sixty or seventy years ago." Then, to change the atmosphere, she put on a cheerful tone reminiscent of a bell ringing and said, "Listen, I'm going to tell you something that will make you laugh a lot; although some events seem funny much later."

Azize then started to tell the story of her mother, Müdrike Hanım, and her stepfather, Nevzat Abi. Her mother needed to find her path in life again, but Azize began by narrating her mother's derailment. According to her story, due to her grandfather's demand that marriage cannot happen before school is finished, her mother and father had agreed to keep their engagement a secret. Since it was also against the rules of the school, her mother wore her engagement ring like a necklace. One day, when her father took his fiancée to their mansion after school, the situation changed. Despite her grandfather's yelling, her mother didn't go back home, which meant that they had to get married immediately. This marked the end of Müdrike's school life. As marriage went on its course, she didn't mind that, but with separation, she realized her mistake. When the children were in middle school, she started attending sewing courses at the community center because she was afraid she would go crazy if she didn't keep herself busy.

Shortly after the divorce, Nevzat Abi appeared. Actually, he was Müdrike's first suitor and a friend of Yusuf from the island.

He proposed to Müdrike, stating that he never gave up loving her. However, Müdrike rejected this proposal, saying that she didn't consider marrying until the twins were fifteen. Nevzat, due to his duties, was stationed in various places and only returned to the island during certain times in the summer. Each time, he repeated his proposal to Müdrike, received the same answer, and left sadly. When their minds finally matured, the girls would joke around by saying, "Look, Mom, Nevzat Abi is here again to propose to you. Should we give him our permission?"

Eventually, on Azize and İmer's fifteenth birthday, Nevzat Abi, who came loaded with gifts, finally succeeded in his endeavor. Müdrike, who had completed the public education course, began working as a sewing teacher for men's underwear at the girls' institute. Her first place of appointment was Ankara, and she went there with her husband, Nevzat Abi. This paved the way for the twins' father to get involved again during their high school years. It led to many other things, both bitter and sweet.

Azize stopped her narration at this point. Her eyes reflected a spark, as if she was grasping something for the first time. She wanted to tell this to Canan right away, "How interesting... I realize that for being ready to compare my mother's marriage decisions and their outcomes with mine, I needed to tell them as a story to someone else. Although the reason I came to life is a result of my father's passionate love, a strong fear must have prevented me from this kind of blindness. I always ran away from such a love. Maybe that's why... On the other hand, my mother's mature love, which would later become her haven, was initially rejected and then accepted as a rational choice. She was at peace ultimately, and we also loved Nevzat Abi and our little brother. This second family of ours always brought us happiness. I can't even imagine a situation where it didn't exist. Rejecting Fahir's love at first and then feeling a deep anxiety within me might be due to the effect of this comparison in my subconscious."

These words struck Canan deeply. She suddenly realized the unspoken question, the underlying emotion that kept her from deciding about marriage, and what she needed to do for the next step. Nevzat Abi or Müdrike Hanım were no longer alive; she couldn't ask them. However, she felt that talking to Fahir would be a big help. Azize would come next. In the course of events, it was he who chose to marry, even knowing full well that she didn't love him with a passionate love. Moreover, she could have decided to ask him about the positive and negative sides of this life they had spent together for nearly fifty years.

Until her next visit, she needed to think about these matters and find a way to spend a long time alone with Fahir, but without tiring him, to understand his perspective on marriage and how these events affected him. This could facilitate Canan's decision. She had these thoughts in mind as she kissed Azize at the door, but left without saying anything to her.

In the days leading up to the next meeting, Canan's mind was preoccupied with finding an opportunity to visit Fahir. However, her workload suddenly intensified, and she found herself struggling to keep up with everything. Her boyfriend even began complaining about her lack of interest, urging her to answer his marriage proposal, and expressing impatience to start their life together and see her prioritize their shared life. The pressure was palpable. Still, Canan knew that there must be an underlying emotion that kept her from deciding, and she sensed that she needed to find and address that emotion before she could take any steps.

The unexpected cancellation of a nearby appointment at the house that Fahir and Azize had used as both a home and an office for many years provided Canan with the opportunity she had been looking for. She was at their door before she had time to ask for their availability in advance. With heart fluttering like a timid fledgling bird, she pressed the doorbell and waited, holding her breath. Sabri opened the door. With his usual silent politeness, he only said, "Please come in," and ushered her inside. At that moment, Canan truly felt like a part of the family. And that she was indeed in the right place to find her way.

When Sabri mentioned that Mr. Fahir would be ready in a little while, Canan instinctively headed to the kitchen, prepared the teapot, and lit the stove. A delightful tea should accompany their conversations. Azize was nowhere around. She must have taken one of her guests to a nearby restaurant. As she disliked going alone, she would take anyone she caught to dine out. She had done so with Canan a few times as well. She remembered their pleasant conversations at that cozy café over filtered coffee and mosaic cake. It was during those meetings that Azize had first mentioned details about her father. Their father had intervened to enroll them in the boarding high school for girls and had then insisted on coming to spend weekends with him and their stepmother. It was clear that he was trying to make up for the past with the hope of compensation. His persistent calls were met with a refusal from both sisters, and they had no enthusiasm to make up for the lost time. Therefore, every weekend, either one of them would fall ill, or one of them would need to study for an exam. In one of their infrequent meetings, they had managed to dissuade their father from leaving the woman for whom he had abandoned their mother. Azize had recounted all this without adding any emotion, as if narrating someone else's story.

Just as Canan was lost in these thoughts, the doorbell rang.

When she realized that she didn't want it to be Azize who was coming, she was surprised. If someone else had come, it would have been worse. Canan had imagined having a leisurely time to talk with Fahir. She waited for Sabri to come and open the door. In the end, it was up to Canan to open the door. When the door opened, she was relieved to find that it was Bilal who had brought their morning orders. After exchanging greetings and small talk, Bilal returned to his work, and Canan busied herself with unpacking the groceries. She smiled when she saw the juicy pears, which seemed like Azize's intuition was at work again, anticipating her visit. She had bitten and chewed on a piece of fruit when Sabri appeared at the kitchen door. With the embarrassment of being caught, she quickly swallowed her bite and looked at Sabri with questioning eyes.

Sabri said, "Mr. Fahri is waiting for you, Miss Canan," and added, "I'll prepare a fruit platter for him. Would you like me to make one for you, too?"

Canan, placing the bitten pear gently on the kitchen counter, said she would appreciate that, turned off the stove where she had placed the teapot, and made her way down the narrow hallway to the room at the end.

Fahir was sitting in the armchair next to the bed. He was wearing his customary attire of a blue short-sleeved shirt, neatly ironed on top of his pajama bottoms. His lap held his daily newspaper, as usual. The fact that the paper was still unopened indicated that he was placing priority on his guest. When he saw Canan, he greeted her with a warm smile. However, a subtle sorrow lingered in his eyes, visible only upon close attention.

Canan sat in the chair adjacent to the one Fahir was sitting in. The chairs were arranged at a slight angle, close enough that their armrests almost touched. She reached out and took both of

Fahir's hands in her own. She squeezed gently, not waiting for him to initiate the gesture. Then she began to softly stroke his hands with her thumbs. The silence between them was comfortable. In a little while, they would have a conversation that was crucial for both.

For Canan, it would address something almost vital, and for Fahir, it would bring to life a plan he had been harboring for some time. Both had come prepared for this meeting. Canan was feeling the pressure of time, knowing she had to ask her questions as soon as possible. Fahir, on the other hand, was eager to talk on marriage with Canan, considering the information Azize had shared with him.

Between the chairs, on the small table, sat a collection of books. When Fahir's eyes wandered to them, Canan's gaze followed. She couldn't help but notice the title of the topmost book, *It's OK Not to Love.* Fahir's name was printed beneath the title. Canan was taken aback and had to suppress the urge to pick up the book. She also felt herself blushing slightly. However, the title of the book seemed to offer her a way into the conversation, so she took the opportunity.

Fahir spoke slowly, giving weight to each word, "When Azize shared the story about the marriage proposal, I wanted you to read my poems. Finish these books and let's see if they're enough."

At that moment, Sabri had brought the fruit platters. Canan didn't touch the plate placed on the side table beside her. Sabri started feeding Fahir the fruits. Knowing that, like everything else, this would also take longer than usual, Canan immersed herself comfortably in the poems in the books.

She started reading from the first book. The first poem had the same title as the book itself. It was truly a poem about loving without expecting anything in return. It said, "Let me love you the way I want and dream; let me work on you like a rare diamond; let me elevate you on the wings of my verses, like a gem on the wings of a bird. My love is enough for both of us; if I love you as much as I want; even if you don't love me, it's fine," it concluded.

She couldn't move on to the next page. The scene Azize had described was etched in her mind. Fahir, who had shrunk when rejected, couldn't possibly be unaware that love doesn't sprout overnight in one's heart like a night's dew. The world had become his. Since he had mentioned that he could love someone else in place of her, he must believe that even if it wasn't a captive love, they could create a mature love by working on it, adding value, dreaming, and infusing it with wings. Canan knew from Azize's stories and her own observations that the two of them had achieved this. She could learn whether she was right or wrong from the other poems. She continued reading.

Shortly thereafter, as Fahir mentioned, "Don't change, stay as you are, and I'll become whatever you wish, a 'great surrender for happiness,'" she realized that it helped Fahir better understand love. Although he could give up himself, it was clear he wouldn't give up Azize. "I can endure anything as long as you stay with me, even if you helplessly leave, take me with you." The poems portrayed various emotions.

On a canvas, words painted an entire life. Friend gatherings, fishing stories, reflections or observations about life, childhood, the unfulfilled life of a young man who lost his father early, love, possibilities, dreams, realities, excitements, pleasures, rebellions, submissions, hope, always hope; and much more...

One poem had the most beautiful expression of gratitude. 'For the love they shared, for embraces, kisses, tears, smiles, shared sleep, sleepless nights, sweet dreams, dreadful thoughts, coquetry, coyness, endless pleasures.' When she read these lines, Canan thought that to appreciate every fragment of shared life, it must be possible only through strong love. Azize's mother had managed to heal the wounds of passionate love only with tranquil love. Somehow, Canan thought that Fahir might also have a deep wound in his past. Just as she was pondering this, the autobiographical poem provided an answer, *"At five, I fell in love / My beloved was twenty years old / Upon hearing the engagement news, I attempted suicide."*

Although she could guess that this could be a memory filled with pain when evaluated with age and experience, Canan found this narrative quite endearing. Maybe it was because she knew Fahir well, so she felt sympathy for his childhood. She felt the urge to embrace that child and say, "It's over, it's all over."

Suddenly, she realized with astonishment that the child was, at the same time, herself. From the age of five to eighteen, she had experienced a one-sided love, and in doing so, she had recalled her fanciful lover, which she had kept a secret from everyone, including the boy himself. When she remembered that she had carried everywhere, she moved the book in which she had dried the poppy he had given her at once, she felt a pain in her heart. As they were childhood friends, she had the right to receive a wedding invitation, but she didn't have the right not to go. It had taken her a long time to overcome this disappointment, and in the end, she had pushed it deep into her memory after labeling it as childish. These memories reminded Canan of the pleasure of passion; also, its tendency to destroy... She decided to think more deeply about this topic later when she was alone.

Canan was reading the poems in the books as if consuming them. A piece of paper on the little table had come into sight when she picked up the last book. Although she glanced at it, she was enthusiastic about reading the next poem. But the paper caught her attention as she was about to put the books back. The shaky handwriting on it reflected the clumsiness of a hand that had to be used later. The books had been presented to her with Fahir's approval, but Canan couldn't be sure whether this paper was included.

When she looked up to ask Fahir, she first noticed that Sabri wasn't there, then her eyes met Fahir's. The eyes that stared at her as if trying to understand what she had felt while she had been lost in the poems signaled a slight nod of approval. Canan reached for the paper, hoping that the most valuable response might be at the end. Each word first imprinted on her mind, then her heart, and finally her soul: *"The knot that tied me to this life has unraveled / Now I am free between existence and non-existence / I left behind loves, passions, hopes / Death blooms in me like a flower."*

While tears welled up in Canan's eyes from the hundreds of verses that had settled within her, she got up, hugged Fahir, and they both cried, trembling. Whether conscious of it or not, their intertwined emotions had become a tangle, holding them together. After a while, the acceptance of the passing years settled into the emptiness that remained. Neither of them could have achieved this alone.

Two weeks had passed. Canan had left Fahir when Azize had not yet returned home. Amid the almost breathless whirlwind they lived in, Canan had briefly spoken with Azize on the phone twice to learn that there were no problems, allowing her to relax and return to her busy routine. In truth, she was eager to share the news with both of them, but she was avoiding doing it over the phone, hoping for a miraculous moment of opportunity to visit them. Finally, when she caught that moment, she rushed to their side. Sabri opened the door. His expression conveyed nothing; he didn't say anything either. He merely stepped aside to make way for Canan to enter the house from the corridor. Despite the darkness of the worst possible scenarios looming within her, Canan raced down the corridor and entered the room at the end.

Fahir was lying in bed. His face was deathly pale. The white sheet covering him was almost indistinguishable from his skin. His eyes were closed, and the gentle rise and fall of his chest indicated his faint breaths. The slow drip of liquid from the serum bottle was decreasing. Azize was by the intravenous stand, adjusting the flow rate and preparing to replace the nearly empty bottle with a full one. She was attempting to conceal a profound sorrow behind a facade of calmness that Canan had never seen before. Azize was diligently attending to her task, becoming once again the physician she had been for years.

Canan's first words were, "Why didn't you inform me? I would have taken you to the hospital." Fahir didn't open his eyes; Azize turned gently toward Canan. She greeted her with a smile that showed her delight at seeing her.

"My dear Canan, Fahir and I have discussed this thoroughly. We won't go to the hospital. This is the best choice for both of us," she said.

Over the next two days, Canan and Azize cared for Fahir as colleagues, and as mother and daughter. With care, tenderness, longing that had been building up for a long time, and gratitude... While the bed sheets and clothes changed, the same cover was always placed over him. Azize told Canan the story behind this cover, which was adorned with rows of lace baskets, like a kind of tapestry, lying over Fahir's chest.

My grandmother used to dress us beautifully so that we

wouldn't feel lacking among the wealthy children of the island. Our clothes, unlike anyone else's, would erase the void left by what they had, but we couldn't approach them. İmer's and my favorite dresses were made of white fabric. Despite being quite simple, the lace baskets lining the skirts lifted them from the ordinary. Within each of these lace baskets, meticulously crafted, were pink, blue, yellow, and purple wildflowers made of lace. It was crucial for us to wear these dresses without staining them. We knew that when they were to be washed, all the lace would be taken off, washed, starched separately, and then sewn back onto the freshly washed and ironed white dresses. From those times, I only have these lace pieces left. They are like symbols of our most beautiful memories. I sewed them onto our first bedsheet when we got married. After using it for a few years, as I was putting it away so as not to wear it out, I thought they would suit my postpartum beds quite well. But it wasn't meant to be. We never used the sheet again. Fahir knew the significance of these lace baskets to me without me having to explain. On our first morning together, he promised as he gently touched the lace that he would make sure to bring the beauties of my childhood days to life, and that he would dedicate his life to spare me even the slightest of pains. He kept that promise more than faithfully. I couldn't put him in any other bed than our wedding bed now.

Canan's hand was on Fahir's pulse constantly. She awaited a moment, a moment she both feared and knew was inevitable. As she noticed Fahir's pulse slowing further, she signaled to Azize that it was time for her to be alone with Fahir. Azize looked at Canan with a watery glint in her sea-blue eyes. She paused, then took a deep breath and whispered, "Canan, I want you to hear what I'm going to say as we say our goodbyes. Your witness to this moment will be the proof that I've lived it from now on."

Canan stood up from the bedside, not forgetting to shake Fahir's left hand and gently stroke it. Moving to the other side of the bed and standing behind Azize, she placed her hands on Azize's shoulders, hoping to lend strength. They stood still, waiting. Canan etched into her mind the words that were spoken as soon as they were audible, *"Is a young soul in an old cage fated to be a bird's destiny? We shared our sorrows, they diminished; we shared our happiness, it grew; we could not share our love, it remained whole."* Canan recognized these lines from poetry books. But the final words were not from any poem, "My Fahir, my love, my life partner, the mountain against which I lean, my lover who soars my heart, I've cherished life with you so much. In my solitude, I'll take haven in what we've lived through, in our memories. I offer a thousand thanks for the lifetime you've dedicated to creating this sanctuary for me..."

The old radio that Fahir carried with him everywhere he went since childhood was continuously turned on to fill the room with sounds while Fahir lay silently on the bed. As the room filled with a special song, *'I entered my beloved's garden, a rosebud amid roses...'* the scent of roses permeated the room. Canan and Azize took their seats in armchairs in the bedroom. One, who had assisted in her arrival to the world, and the other, who had transformed her world into heaven, fixed their gazes on the man they loved. They waited. When the song ended, Azize reached for the old radio to turn it off. The old radio fell silent, and so did the room. The women, too. The lace baskets, already moving, slowly stopped.

Disenchantment

"Now, if he were to take my hand and lead me away, I would go with him. In fact, I yearn for him to do it. Yet just this morning, I was complaining to you, wasn't I? I remember it all. Moreover, I said it all with conviction. Don't worry, I am in control of myself. But what is this fluttering feeling?" she said and fell silent. I had no response to give. Apparently, she wasn't expecting to be comforted or to hear my opinion. After a brief silence, she continued speaking, "Do you know I resisted for years? Because I thought we had no future together, I kept telling myself and him about the impossibility of a relationship between us. 'Forget it, child,' I said, 'we can't be a couple.' But now I see how intertwined our lives are. Not only am I not bothered by it, but I also haven't even realized."

I had known both for a short time. I first met Gamze—that's another story. We had coincided with each other frequently in this short time and because we worked on some projects together; we had grown fond of each other. I heard the name Yusuf from her often. "Yusuf will come for dinner tonight," "Yusuf will bring me to you tomorrow," "I left my dress at the tailor's; Yusuf will pick it up after work…" They weren't married. I knew Gamze lived alone. Moreover, to my knowledge, she had never been married before. They were not business partners. They didn't even work in the same field. They couldn't be schoolmates either because Yusuf had to be a few years younger than Gamze. Apart from this, I don't know much about their relationship. As a matter of fact, I don't ask or question anyone's life. If someone wants to tell, they can. If not, they don't have to. In both cases, I did what I felt was necessary. When asked, only as much as necessary, I express my opinion. That way, my mind remains clear. In short, only after Gamze chose to share I learn something about them.

"Our encounter was a strange coincidence that I don't remember the details of. Now I see that we have gradually become more supportive of each other in various matters. Unknowingly, without realizing it, we have become a team. The ordinary events of daily life start earlier every day. It's not just with me; Yusuf is also accustomed to the routines of my family members. At least twice a week, he visits my mother in the morning and discusses current economic news over coffee. My father's newspaper is delivered to the office by Yusuf. My niece Sude calls him to pick her up after her classes, not me."

I had no idea why she was telling me all of this. We were driving in her car from Izmir to a meeting in Ankara. This trip wasn't related to either of our jobs; we were going to bring together a few people for the first stage of a social responsibility project. Since we had been discussing this topic almost until the early hours of the morning for the past few days, she must have wanted to divert our attention to another direction during the journey. She would often talk about something called "business blindness," where people become unable to see problems when they are too immersed in a subject. In such cases, it is beneficial to step outside and then return. If Gamze wanted to choose a topic that was completely opposite to our project for our road trip conversation, it could only be about our personal lives. The fact that we had never discussed each other's personal lives before and that she thought it was time for our relationship to evolve into a more friendly one seemed like another reason. If she wanted me to give advice, she couldn't do it by beating around the bush. I felt the need to say something encouraging.

"He's a really good person; at least that's what I've seen. It seems like having someone who supports you like that makes life easier."

"He really is a very good person. That has been the most impressive aspect of him since we met. It's as if he's always ready to do good for others. Sometimes, I find this attitude to be too much. I even think it's a degree of naivety. When I see him being taken advantage of, it drives me crazy, but his reaction is always very calm: *What's the matter?* He believes every experience has a reason behind it. According to him, they wouldn't happen if there weren't a lesson for him to learn. The fact that we have such different aspects sometimes drives me crazy. While I become disillusioned with life and people, even with the slightest negativity, he embraces everything wholeheartedly. I even think he silently appreciates the obstacles he encounters. And because of this, while I am restless, he is incredibly calm, relaxed, and free of worry."

"The things you're saying about him, in my opinion, are good qualities. But according to your description, it's as if the guy is the most stolid person in the world."

"Come on, I actually like this attitude of him."

"Then, you envy it."

"What is there to envy? I could never do that. Everything should be under my control. I say, 'The guy is relaxed.' How can you trust someone like that?"

"When you say trust, what exactly do you mean?"

"I mean, how can you entrust your future to him?"

"Oh, my… Is this Yusuf of yours a thief, liar, someone who

mistreats others, and abandons his companions?"

"He doesn't do any of those things. If he were like that, I would never allow him to be around me or my family. Honesty, loyalty, and faithfulness are very important qualities to me. I chose all my friends based on these criteria. I also strive to always embody those qualities myself. If someone makes a mistake, I wipe them from my life. Yusuf has passed all these tests."

"Living in such a 'either always or never' manner must be exhausting."

"Why did you say that?"

"The more you say 'never' and 'always,' that's how I feel. They call it neurosis, you know?"

"Oh, come on. Now you've declared me a neurotic woman."

"The source of this situation is the voice buzzing inside a person. It's not just in you, it's in me, too. But ever since I became aware of it, I've been working on reducing it. Not long ago, about five years ago, I was just like you. I had a few friends who held a mirror up to me. I think I've come a long way. Now, it seems it's my turn. For the first time, I see how clearly you're perceived from the outside, but it goes unnoticed when you're living it, and it's even accepted naturally."

We were so engrossed in our conversation that I suddenly realized we were in the car when the driver said, "Apologies for interrupting, Ms. Gamze. You had asked me to let you know if there's a nice place to stop before reaching Afyon." We had stopped by the side of the road.

As someone who had traveled the Izmir-Ankara road multiple times by bus, I had seen a few rest stops with a gas station and a restaurant. But since they were not particularly beautiful or special, I didn't want to stop at any of them. Even though I thought about saying, *Let's keep going without stopping,*

I remained silent because I was just a guest on this journey. On the other hand, a cup of tea with a single slice of lemon in a large glass mug, without sugar, wouldn't be bad at all. Plus, we could stretch our numb legs a bit by taking a walk.

While I was thinking, the driver continued, "I couldn't find a place where you would be comfortable around here. However, I noticed a cluster of willow trees on the side of this closed gas station. Look right across. If you like, we can stop there. Just in case, I put your camping chairs in the trunk and a few items that I thought might be useful."

Both Gamze and I sparkled with excitement. We looked at each other and conveyed our approval with our smiles to the person in front of us. Gamze said, "Well then, show us your skills, Mehmet. You're going to pull a rabbit out of a hat, I guess."

Mehmet started the car and slowly drove toward the cluster of willow trees. He stopped a little further away. It turned out that he did this to set up the chairs under the tree. While we wandered around a bit to relieve the numbness in our feet, he made the preparations. When we returned, I couldn't believe my eyes. Gamze, on the other hand, greeted the view as if it was ordinary; it was clear that she had witnessed similar situations before.

Two camping chairs were placed side by side but slightly turned toward each other in the shade of the tree. This way, when we sat down, we could see each other from the side. However, the striking part of the preparation was not this thoughtfulness. On the makeshift table made from a tree stump placed right in front, there was a thermos and two empty glass cups. It was a big surprise to me.

"How did you manage this?" I asked Mehmet, and he explained briefly, saying, "There is a kettle that could take electricity from the car lighter." He used it to prepare hot water, put the tea bag in the thermos, and added water. Our tea was left to steep, waiting for us. When we sat on our chairs, Mehmet filled the cups with tea. Then I saw him holding a lemon. And then, with a pocketknife, he cut the lemon in half...

He put one half on the small plate between our glasses and prepared small lemon slices from the edge of the other half, placing them on the plate as well. He also opened a package of whole wheat biscuits with sultanas and placed it on the table. When he asked if we had any other requests, I was still looking at his face in astonishment. I said, "Thank you, Mehmet," and thought to myself while examining his face to see, *Could he have heard what I had in mind just before the break?* Then, of course, I laughed to myself. I decided to stop playing and enjoy this surprise tea.

The branches of the willow tree were dancing in front of our eyes with a gentle breeze. I enjoyed listening to the rustling sound they made. Just then, Mehmet turned toward the car and moved away from us. Gamze resumed the conversation where we had left off.

"Before the break, you diagnosed me with neurosis."

"I'm not a psychiatrist, dear Gamze. Moreover, what I said doesn't carry a diagnostic nature. I was trying to explain a personality trait by giving an example from myself."

"Don't think that I took offense or got hurt. Actually, what you said resonated with me, that's why I'm repeating it. I know very well what you mean by the buzzing sound inside me. Is there a way to silence it? If there is, please tell me so that it can be complete."

"It doesn't stop, but we can try not to hear it. It's a skill that develops as you make peace with yourself. To make peace, we need to get to know ourselves. Getting to know ourselves can only happen by exploring within. They are all interconnected."

"Have you succeeded?"

"I'm still working on it."

"Then let me start somewhere, too. Will you explain to me how to do it?"

"First question; is my life the way I want it to be?"

This question caused a relatively long silence in the conversation. I was expecting that. It wasn't a question that could be answered immediately, and it was the kind of question that would set many thought gears in motion while searching for an answer. I knew that from my own experience. It had come to my mind on the eve of my fortieth birthday, gnawed at my brain, and turned my life upside down, and as I realized that the bottom might be better than the top, the process entered a calmer phase. Five years had passed since then. The most important reason for the tranquility that settled in my soul was the dozens of steps I had taken to live the life I wanted. I still had a long way to go. As I contemplated this, I thought that we still had a long way to go to reach Ankara. I looked at Gamze; she seemed restless too. She got up without saying a word, and then I got up as well. Mehmet, who saw us in this state, quickly came over to us. He had collected our belongings and passed us while we were walking to the car. When we settled into our seats in the back, the trunk closed, and Mehmet took his place. We set off. None of us made a sound. After a while, Gamze was the first to speak.

"Bahar, where did you find that heavy question? My soul will crack while searching for the answer, not my brain. It wasn't such a clear thought. My life just passed through my mind like a filmstrip. Various scenes and moments illuminated my eyes as if forcing them upon me, without any criteria for ordering. For example, childhood memories are interrupted by a recent event. At one moment, I saw how my father motivated me with his love in every aspect of life. In the next moment, I realized that I imposed the same shackles on myself, silencing the storms inside me just to hear a single word of approval from my mother. I started to think that I let all the men I reached the stage of marriage into my life because they resembled my father, but I turned away from them at the last moment because I felt they couldn't love me as much as my father did. In this short period, you presented me with the unresolved confrontations of so many years. Will it be worth it, given how overwhelmed I feel? At what stage are you in this reckoning? Where will it end? Tell me that at least."

"Let me tell you this much; we are not the first or the last people to start this questioning. Moreover, through this process, we can interpret events that come our way differently and extract valuable lessons from them. We can make sense of what happens to us. These inquiries are crowned with many realizations that may not hold much value until we share them with others."

"I think I'm beginning to understand. You're a healer. Otherwise, why would you appear in front of me at the most critical turning point in my life?"

"Are you saying this because of the meeting in Ankara and the project you will dive into afterward?"

"No, dear, that will happen somehow. Work and similar things are my unquestionable dominions. I have been working for so long that my nature has evolved in that direction somehow. I feel comfortable and safe there. My soft spot is emotional relationships."

For a moment, I blurted out, "Right, we were talking about Yusuf. We ended up here," and at the same time, I covered my mouth with my hands like trying to stop my sayings and looked at Mehmet. It was as if we were on my living room sofa, not in the back seat of the car. I had recklessly delved into the most private topic. Moreover, I, who boasted about not prying into anyone's private life, had done it. Apologetically, I looked at Gamze. She smiled understandingly.

"If you knew the kind of private matters I discuss with Mehmet, you wouldn't be so flustered," she said, soothing me. She continued, "He doesn't listen, and even if he hears, he doesn't retain it. Being privy to many secrets is inherent in being a private chauffeur. Therefore, those who are trustworthy are accepted. Mehmet is one of the best in this business. I'm really curious about your impression of Yusuf. Come on, start. I can't wait any longer to hear."

"My dear Gamze, I don't know how to say it. It feels like I'm crossing the line, especially as someone who has always made it a principle not to meddle in anyone's business. I'm also afraid of being misunderstood."

"Bahar, please don't... I feel like I'm going to burst because of your delicate and careful attitude."

"It wasn't my intention to flatter you. OK, then I'll tell you what I'm thinking. Throughout my life experiences and observations of people, I have seen many individuals who act as if they are unaware of being married and lead various, quote-unquote, free lives. But for the first time, I see two people who think they are not married and are actually unaware that they are married."

"Oh, my... I never looked at it that way."

"At least that's my impression. And I think what you refer to as a turning point revolves around the question, 'Should I marry Yusuf?'"

"According to you, this question has already been answered, right?"

"I know that marriage is more than the moments I've seen you together or the sharing I've heard from you. If you don't agree with my interpretation of your relationship, you need to pinpoint what is missing. That way, you can see where you need to go and also question whether you truly want to go there."

"You turned me into an interrogator."

"Is that so bad?"

"We'll see. If things become completely tangled in relationships and emotions, I hope you'll lend a hand."

"As much as I can… But I know that you will break free from your cocoon without needing anyone. Like a caterpillar becoming a butterfly. If they emerge from their cocoon with the help of others, their struggle for life is incomplete, and butterflies cannot become strong. Gamze, think about it. If it wasn't time for you to question your life, my few words on this matter would have been in vain. We would spend the journey discussing tomorrow's project meeting. You wouldn't push yourself to find an answer to my question."

"You're right. There's an excitement inside me that I can't define. I'm eagerly anticipating what will happen."

"You need time. The question has been asked once. It depends on you to find clarity within yourself during this time."

"I think I understand what you mean, but don't forget to nudge me occasionally! There's always a risk of taking the easy way out. After all, self-scrutiny is not something one eagerly does, let alone sustains."

"Don't worry; I'm here."

"You'll stay, right?"

"Of course. I should take responsibility for the processes I have initiated."

At the end of the road, which we didn't realize how time passed while talking, we arrived in front of the hotel in Ankara and snapped back to reality. It was late. We went to the hotel restaurant to eat something and then to our rooms to rest. I fell asleep immediately, but I had no doubt that Gamze was contemplating our conversation and reflecting on different periods of her life based on that.

The next day's meeting was a complete success. As she had said, she had an unwavering professionalism. Her success lay in anticipating disagreements during the meeting and preventing them from escalating into complications. She played a significant role in ensuring that both parties committed to the goal we set during our conversation in creating the project, as if it were their own objectives.

She had to return immediately. As for me, while I was in Ankara, I didn't want to leave without seeing a few dear friends and experiencing some enjoyable moments that I would like to repeat, so I stayed for one more day. Thus, throughout the entire workday and on the return journey, we didn't have the opportunity to discuss the previous topic. When I returned to Izmir, I couldn't meet Gamze because she was busy with business meetings in other cities. At least ten days had passed since then. During this time, we could only communicate through short text messages. I was very curious about how she was doing. She hadn't made any sound for the past two or three days.

I had been preparing for my first camping experience alone for several months. I had converted my 1969 model Volkswagen T2 minibus into a livable space, realizing my dream of having a small kitchen corner and a sofa-like rear seat, resembling a member of the turtle family. All that remained was to park my campervan wherever I wanted and fully set up the camping equipment. My camping chairs and foldable table, hammock, and the rainbow-colored puzzle-patterned curtain to cover the front window were waiting for this moment.

I imagined a camping spot near the sea, but also adjacent to the forest. However, that required more relaxed times, like summer vacation. Even so, I had to wait for two more months. The small cabinets and drawers in my kitchen were filled with all kinds of utensils for cooking and eating. I had thought about every possible need in detail and collected miniature versions of many items from different stores over the years. Even though I hadn't obtained my dream campervan yet, gathering all these things in one corner could be called "sending a message to the universe," I suppose.

Ultimately, I was ready to chase my dreams. However, I couldn't go alone, and I couldn't wait for the right time to go to the seaside. That's because Gamze called me one midnight in a panic and said, "Please come and take me from here; I can't breathe."

The next day, around noon, we got into the campervan and hit the road. She didn't ask where we were going, but I knew. After hanging up the phone at night, I had done some search on the internet. I had chosen a destination where we could stay at least one night, both talking and enjoying the silence, purifying our souls. It was also a place where we could embrace nature in one of the paradises on Earth; Lake Salda. It was recommended to those curious about unworldly stories, because the lake was famous for its white sands thought to originated from planet Mars. For me, even being a volcanic crater lake added great mystery to it, and I had read many captivating comments about it on various travel pages. Its inclusion in the world heritage conservation made it the most appealing aspect to me. Moreover, after examining the photographs in the visuals section, our route became clear. We had approximately a four-hour journey from Izmir to Denizli, and then to Lake Salda. It would take a bit longer with the campervan, but what mattered was being on the road—which I constantly reiterated—it wasn't a problem, but an opportunity. I had made my travel plans with an indisputable determination, and I had decided to start the journey in the morning without allowing Gamze to comment. While I woke up early and was prepared, I was thinking about it. Anyway, poor Gamze had no intention of making any comments.

I went to pick her up. When she opened the door, she was silent like a figurine, lifeless as if the death sentence had just been read. I had told her on the phone, "Just pack a few clothes and a thick tracksuit."

She had prepared a small bag. Taking it from her, I gently guided her toward the campervan, holding her by her left elbow. I felt the need to open the door for her. She sat herself on the front seat like a solid block. Faintly, she murmured, "I'm ready." Her voice was set to be so low and colorless that it seemed to be deliberately suppressing the continuation of the conversation; I was grateful for that. Trying to delve into her inner world and lead her out of the maze where she seemed lost, in a conversation where I didn't know where to begin, seemed daunting to me. I focused solely on the road. Turning on the radio was a habitual act during my journeys, and it was done spontaneously, without much thought. On the other hand, it might have been useful not to further burden the silence. The reason I chose the radio instead of listening to songs in a pre-determined order like an album was that I wanted the songs to be a surprise. The occasional conversations with the program guests gave me the feeling of having many companions on my journey. Especially this time. I needed that feeling more than before because, even though Gamze's body was with me, who knows where her mind was? I might have left her in a soundless void, and that made me uneasy. However, what was right was to start preparing our settlement and dealing with the situation from the very beginning, when we reached the end of the road. The feeling inside me said that this trip would be beneficial for both of us in different ways.

I entered a gas station at the Cankurtaran junction as we left Denizli. I filled up the tank and bought a five-liter bottle of water. After paying at the cash register, I noticed the fruit stand in front of the market. It was the cherry season. The cherries in this region were delicious. I had a kilogram weighed. I thought about buying them to take home if we returned from this direction. I said, "If we return," because I sometimes developed an obsession with not turning back from the path I had taken. Everyone has their quirks, after all.

According to the sign for Lake Salda, it was time to find where we would camp after taking the approximately one-hour gravel road from the junction as indicated on the same sign. The camping site owned by the Yeşilova Municipality was highly recommended in travel articles on the internet. It was especially important that we could have an electricity connection. Although I had been running the small refrigerator on the road through the accumulator and managed to keep our food healthy, it wouldn't be sufficient for the entire camping duration. Additionally, I needed electricity for my small electric radio and, if necessary, for a handheld fan. With the long yellow cable, I plugged into the socket next to the engine. I could get city electricity from the outside. This was the most urgent task for the camping.

I told Gamze, "Sit here for a while; I'll take care of the

electricity and set up the chairs and the table. Once we regain our composure, we can set up your tent." And that's what I did. I opened the tent opposite the minibus's pop-up door. It was one of those easily opened two-person tents. I placed an inflatable mattress inside and quickly inflated it with an electric compressor.

Normally, when dealing with such things with someone next to me, it would annoy me if they didn't even lift a finger and I would definitely say something to them, urging them to do their own work. But this couldn't be applied to Gamze because her face revealed her depression. Her generally silent demeanor and the slow, soft way she spoke a few words were reflections of her state. Especially when compared to her previous states...

Occasionally, memories of our trip to Ankara and the process I triggered to increase her self-awareness came to my mind, and when I thought about the possibility that this state might be a consequence of it, I felt constricted. It was important to settle in quickly, not to be left in the dark, and to start getting Gamze to talk as soon as possible. It happened as I had planned.

She resisted until we started talking at the dinner table. I tried to engage her in conversation by talking about this and that. I could see that she was more open compared to when we arrived. The night sky was covered with stars. The moon's brightness was falling onto the lake. I cooked meatballs with a little oil in a Teflon pan and placed them between bread slices, accompanied by a shepherd salad with plenty of ingredients, pomegranate molasses, olive oil, and ready-made *ayran* (a yogurt-based drink). While we were having dinner, we talked about various topics. I washed the cherries and placed them on the table. I took a deep breath.

We were sitting in the dark, with no light other than the

moon. It was an environment that would facilitate discussing serious matters. Instead of playing games, I realized it would be better to clearly express what I expected from her. So, I started, "Gamze, you wanted me to take you away. Without questioning, I brought you here. There was a cry for help in your voice. Now we're here; it's just the two of us. In order for me to fulfill that expectation, you need to open up to me. What's going on? Why have you closed yourself off to such an extent? The lively businesswoman, my friend whom I've grown accustomed to seeing, what happened that caused you to fall into depression?"

She started to talk hesitantly. "Bahar, I don't know where to start. If I knew, you would be the one I would tell. The person who could help me…"

"During the ten days we didn't see each other, you must have experienced something; start from there. I stayed in Ankara, and you returned to Izmir. You informed me about your meetings in other cities through text messages. You didn't tell me how you were doing. But something negative must have happened, right? Or did a sudden event completely shatter you?"

"My mother… My mother has pneumonia. She's at home, not in the hospital… I couldn't go to her. You know how busy my work is. When I found out from my sister that my mother was fine and they didn't need to hospitalize her, I decided that when I found a suitable opportunity, as soon as possible, I would go to her. She said, 'Don't come, she must have important things to do now.' If someone else said that, you wouldn't doubt that it meant exactly what it was said, but when it's about my mother, it's as heavy as saying 'don't even come to my death.' It's an expression that shows disappointment. Even if I had gone, I wouldn't have been able to mend things. She always says that my work is very important, and I learned to be uncompromising in my work from her. I am my mother's daughter."

"You are your mother's daughter, yes. But it's not a bad thing to be our mothers' daughters. We just need to fight the battles we couldn't fight with them ourselves. For our future daughters…"

"Why do you think I'm afraid of getting married and having children? In fact, I would have loved to have a daughter. A son, and then a daughter. So that my daughter could seek refuge with her brother. Actually, I still want that. Time is passing. Soon I won't have a chance; I'm about to lose my chance of having a child without taking major health risks."

"I thought being a successful businesswoman was important to you. Before we met, I heard from a few people who talked about how ambitious you were."

"I was like that, but now I'm not sure what I expect from life. It might not just be about career success. I have a job and opportunities that many people would envy, but why is it not enough to make me happy?"

"It would be enough if you were someone who was content."

"Tell me why I can't be content, then."

"How can I know that? Only you can find this information about yourself. If you don't know it now, it must be somewhere within you."

"My life is like cheese stuck in water; it appears solid and whole, but it's actually soft and easily falls apart. It's not worth holding on to… When you touched me while going to Ankara, look where it led us. While living my life, I suddenly stopped and realized that I've been living, working, and planning my future based on the guidance of others for years. I also understood that it's wrong, but I can't find what to do to change it."

"The rule of nature works with the cycle of 'growth,

transformation, and continuation.'"

"Even if it causes pain?"

"It's not about the pain you feel; I know that's how it seems to you right now. I went through a similar turning point myself. I'm sure many people are struggling, just like us. When we reach a certain point, we can better understand how much time is left and the importance of spending it the way we truly want, as our authentic selves."

"So, do you believe I can find my way?"

"I believe in you. And I'll do whatever I can to help you with that. Just do the same. I struggled with these things alone. I asked myself the same question, "Which one am I? What I've done, what I've dreamed of doing, or worse, what I've given up dreaming?" If we had met five years ago, you would understand what I mean. Now I realize that you're my turning point. You're my midlife crisis. If I could help you go through this process more easily, I won't have wasted those years of questioning and beyond."

"I'm not calling you a healer for no reason. Look at how I've come here and how I feel now. It's like you have a magic wand; you're good for me. You wouldn't have brought me here if we wouldn't find answers. That's why I want to sleep now and look forward to tomorrow with hope. In fact, I want to find rest in that hope."

I wished Gamze a good night's sleep and went to my bed in the caravan. I wanted to pull her out of the state of mind she was in and was searching for ways to do it. But I suddenly realized how much I raised her expectations and how she could fall apart if I couldn't meet them. That's what disturbed my sleep. I tossed and turned for a while, but I had such a tiring day that I fell asleep without realizing it. I woke up early with the sunlight shining into my eyes. I hadn't thought of closing the curtains with all those thoughts in my head during the night. Fortunately, there were no other campers besides us. When I looked outside, I saw Gamze sitting in the camping chair where she spent the night. She had turned toward the lake, her back facing me.

I encouraged myself, *Come on, Bahar, you've taken on a challenging guidance task. But you'll see that you'll succeed.* As soon as I said that, I shivered, because what would be the indicator of success? The possibility of failure suddenly squeezed my chest, as if saying, "I'm here too." I couldn't know the result without trying. Moreover, I had allowed the road to bring us here without a definite plan. Letting oneself go with the flow... I hoped life had a plan.

"Good morning, Gamze dear, how are you this morning?"

I said as I got out of the caravan. She turned slightly toward me, turning her head to look at me, and said with excitement, "Excited. How else should I feel on the day I will find answers to my questions?" She smiled a bit wistfully. There was irony in her voice, or at least that's how it seemed to me, but I smiled widely. Just to contaminate her with it...

Gamze wanted to get a brief breakfast. I found this proposition unacceptable.

I had made many preparations. The honey and clotted cream duo were prepared in one bowl, in an amount suitable for one breakfast. The goat cheese needed to be served with pink tomatoes. The walnut kernels to be sprinkled on top were waiting in their packets. The pomegranate juice, taken out of the freezer and left to thaw in the refrigerator, had turned out to be perfect for our taste. Two organic eggs were waiting in a pan, and a piece of butter was ready to cook them sunny side up.

"You wander around; the table will be ready in half an hour.

We'll start such a day with a breakfast that befits it. That's it..."

I moved Gamze away from me, as she seemed to be muttering. When the table was almost ready, I saw her running toward me, screaming. I worried if she had been bitten by some bug. But she came to me, and with excitement, she started telling me.

"Bahar, I couldn't believe my eyes. You'll go crazy when you hear it too. Oh, if only I had seen it when we arrived yesterday, I could never stay here. The whole camp is infested. Hazel mice are running wild everywhere. I saw mice poking their heads out and then quickly running back into their holes; dozens of mice... Some of them were even darting from hole to hole. I'm sure their empire covers the underground. Who knows how many layers are beneath the ground... I've never seen anything like this before. And I slept in a tent... What if they got inside... What if they did... *Yuck!*... Tell me you didn't know about this. If you knew and hid it from me, I will never forgive you!"

I didn't know. Even if I did, I wouldn't have cared; but if I could have predicted that it would cause Gamze to recover from the dullness of depression so quickly, I would have adjusted the dosage of fear explosion before coming this far. I felt like laughing, but I couldn't laugh. Still, I shared my observation, reducing the mocking tone to ensure that she confronts her situation, "Gamze Sultan, I can see that the adrenaline released by a few mice has improved your mood. You won't sulk in silence anymore."

She suddenly paused in her excited state and looked at me. I guess she was trying to figure out if I was serious or not. Apparently, she couldn't tell, so she asked me.

"Yes," I said, "I'm very serious. Why wouldn't I be? Look at how lively you've become. Come on, our breakfast is ready. The finest... Sit and let's eat. We still have unanswered questions."

I handed her one of the mica cups that I had divided the crimson pomegranate juice into, and I raised the other one. "To inner peace! If it's there, everything is OK," I said.

Gamze also raised her cup and said, "To inner peace!"

Breakfast was finished by eleven o'clock. We cleaned the plates at the nearby fountain and left them there. We would do the proper washing later. By that time, I had already managed to restrain Gamze. She was whining with childish self-centeredness, saying, "Let's just do whatever we're going to do already."

Actually, there was a reason for my slowness; I didn't know what to do. Suddenly, the thought of going to the edge of the water came to my mind. How could I not have thought of it before? I had read that this area, known as the Maldives of Turkey, got its name from its white sand and turquoise water. It was said to be the deepest lake in our country. I had also seen warnings about its swamp-like effect due to its clay-like soil, which could suck things in.

Although the sun was high up, the air was cool. Therefore, I informed Gamze that we would take a walk by the lake without mentioning wearing swimsuits. In fact, I had said it in a rather formal tone. I managed to make her walk beside me without objecting. Gamze suddenly stopped. We were going to pass through the mice's paradise. Even though I first said, "Come on, walk, as if it's medicine," I couldn't bring myself to do it. After scanning the surroundings, I chose to go toward the facility on our side and reach the lakeshore through the stony path in front of it. We were walking in silence. I wanted to talk, but I couldn't find the right words for that moment. It felt like my bag was empty.

On the other hand, Gamze's restlessness had subsided. She wasn't opening her mouth either. *Let's walk for a while and see,* I thought to myself. I started to enjoy the walk on the white sand that I could describe as specks of gravel dust. I had tied my sandals together and hung them over my shoulder. The turquoise color of the lake had lost its intensity in the sunlight, but we didn't care at that moment because our eyes were fixed on the sand. We both walked with our heads bowed. With the same steps, catching the same pace... Like experiencing what comes our way in an unknown ritual...

Suddenly, I saw a gray insect remnant at the tip of my toe. I call it a remnant because it was no longer an insect. The only surprising thing about what remained was that it was just a shell. The gray color might not have stood out among the white sands if it hadn't been so shiny. What made it unexpected was that there was no trace of the former insect's body inside the shell, as if it had been abandoned without ever showing any signs of life. I showed it to Gamze, but she acted disinterested. We continued our walk. The same pace, heads bowed.

Soon, it was Gamze who reached out her arm to stop me. I looked at where she was pointing. I thought it was another shell. It was, with one difference; there was a living creature trying to come out of it. I was left in awe, my mouth slightly open. Gamze was no different. The shell was brown, not gray, but it was the same size and shape as the previous one. The body was motionless on the sand. The three pairs of legs, typical of arthropods, were motionless on either side. But the head was protruding forward. The neck had elongated, managing to pull a part of the body out of the shell. Apparently, as we observed, this insect gave birth to itself with its head remaining the same, leaving behind its old body and replacing it with a new one.

A miracle was happening before our eyes, and this transformation was taking place very slowly. We were going to wait motionless, but when we saw another empty gray shell next to it, and another bug that had almost completely emerged from its shell about half a meter away, we started to move slowly. With the increase in heat, dozens of new brown bugs started to emerge from the lake. We were able to observe the whole process from the initiation of transformation to the final stage, in multiple separate scenes, watching the before and after phases. I thought it resembled a known insect, but I couldn't figure out which one.

While watching the part up to here repeatedly, we had been moving rapidly and with a movement resembling crawling on the sand. Under the reflecting effect of white light, we began to feel that the parts of our bodies exposed to the sun's heat were burning considerably. Even if we were to return with the bronze tan known as "worker's burn," we didn't care.

The new bodies had wings in all insects. The initially wrinkled and folded wings were gradually extending further. There was no compromise on motionless waiting at any stage. I had started to feel uncomfortable with the subtle sting of the burn. Suddenly, I exclaimed, "It's a dragonfly! It's the very one. Do you know that, Gamze?" We couldn't leave without seeing at least one dragonfly flying.

To trigger its flight, I started throwing pebbles near it, clapping my hands, and making noise. It didn't move. Then, unexpectedly, it took off. Buzzzz. Apparently, its wings, like silk pelerine, had dried enough, and it had become capable of flying. Since we had reached the end of our documentary, we immediately stood up. When we started walking back toward the shade, neither of us was talking. I thought Gamze was going through the entire process in her mind, putting it in order, and trying to make sense of it. I let her be, to be at ease.

We had returned to our campsite. Our table and camping chairs were still in place as we had left them. They were ready for us to discuss the matter in detail. I decided to wait for Gamze to start the conversation. Meanwhile, I accessed the internet on my phone and read about the life cycle of a dragonfly, examining its visuals. What we had seen was biologically real and accurate. I realized that we had achieved a comprehensive opportunity for observation. But how could we find out if it had any intellectual implications? I kept replaying in my mind both our observations in real-time and the sequential footage in the internet video. That's when Gamze initiated the dialog with a question.

"Do you think I'm OK?"

"In what sense?"

"Life…"

"Think about yourself and say the first word that comes to your mind; I'll decide based on that."

"Joy!"

"It's a wonderful sign; if that's the word you used to define yourself, you must be doing well in life."

"Then why am I not aware of it?"

"Don't you keep saying it? The reason is 'business blindness.' Step out and take a look from the outside; you'll see what I see."

"You're hitting me with my own words. You're smart. I'm glad I don't have you as a competitor in the workplace. You could have easily overshadowed me!"

"I love being a literature teacher. While everyone was studying business, I left Marmara Business School at the end of my second year, having passed the finals. I had taken the exam that year to be able to go to the Faculty of Education. When I found out I got in, I didn't think twice and changed my faculty. So, I'm not your competitor."

"How did we get here? I think it originated from me constantly judging myself in recent days."

"'When you can't find anyone to judge, you judge yourself, and that's the hardest of all,' says the King in the book The Little Prince. "

"Well, why can't he find anyone to judge? Is he alone? Can't he bear it?"

"He is alone in the midst of crowds; he doesn't feel loneliness in his heart. And it's not about 'not being able to' bear it; it's the childlike belief, mixed with adult idealism, that everyone should judge themselves."

"I thought these things only happened in books or movies. The girl's life is messy; one day a healer appears. They slowly begin to unravel it like a ball of yarn. The girl is not scared but full of fear, not dead but full of death, surrounded by people but alone. The healer is calm, with the wisdom of years, holding reason in one hand and heart in the other, clear and cool like water."

"Do you know what I think about you as I get to know you?"

"I'd give anything to hear that…"

"You have lived for others to the extent of not knowing what you love. You have mistreated yourself, even let others mistreat you. While you long for unconditional love, you have been tested with love offered only as a reward. You have put your work above everything out of fear that you would fall if you stopped. You have set goals, achieved them, and immediately set new ones. But if you become too successful, you have believed that people will love you. Maybe you have been made to believe that. Did I go too far? Why are you crying?"

"Don't mind me. I've been like this lately. I've become teary-eyed. I can't hold myself back. Actually, I'm not even trying to hold myself back these days. Crying is related to the 'secret' behind the mirror. When tears flow, the secret disappears. Glass emerges; my inner self is revealed."

"Then let me say this last thing; let my evaluation be complete. You will leave your past self behind. Your old body will remain as a dry shell. You will be the one drying your wings. Don't forget that."

"There's a strange, new me inside. Pure, a bit foolish, but bouncing and smiling like a child. You must have sent it, it's enveloping me like a vine. And it's pink. One end is blue too; like the sea, like rain, or the color of a baby boy's onesie."

"When I said you would dry your wings, let me share it with you too. While reflecting on our observations by the lakeside earlier, I realized that I could interpret them with two concluding sentences. One, you can always give birth to a new version of yourself. Two, you can only fly when your wings are dry."

Gamze remained silent for a while and then repeated in a low voice, "I can always give birth to a new version of myself, and I can only fly when my wings are dry."

She looked at me as if asking if she had understood correctly. Her gaze was so childlike and vulnerable that I went over and hugged her on the chair she had sat down. I stroked her back from top to bottom once. It was a symbolic gesture, as if saying, "Can I help you shed some of your burdens?" She must have sensed her intention. She let out a sigh of relief. I straightened up.

"I'm glad we came here," I said.

But her mind was working differently. She said a little embarrassedly, "It has definitely done me good, but you didn't benefit from this." I talked in the right mind.

"Although I didn't try to support you with an expectation of gain, I must say that I have gained significant insights from what I said, the interpretations I made, and what I have realized about my own life while observing your introspection. Building up this accumulation over the years certainly came at a cost. Every choice was a sacrifice. Yes, I have accumulated things in my baggage, but I forgot to ask myself, 'Am I happy with them now?' I haven't tried to find what I would want to change. I'm telling you, have I been able to give myself my final form? Is there another self, waiting to emerge within me?"

"There is a statement that says, "Just as I found all the right answers, they changed the questions." Ours is a similar case…"

"Now, after all this, look inside yourself; tell me what you see without mixing in new questions."

"If you remember, this started when we questioned the point we reached with Yusuf. I thought about these things while lying down last night. Maybe because my wings are starting to dry, I can see certain things more clearly now. Although I love him, the reason I couldn't bring him into my life was because I knew he wouldn't fit the life goals my parents set for me. They love him a lot, but they don't find him suitable as a partner for me. He is not strong and easily gets emotional. He doesn't know strategic planning; he speaks or acts without thinking. However, we have a lot of unwritten family rules. We live within certain patterns. I have accepted getting stuck there without complaining. The way you approached it made me realize that I had taken over other people's lives. I guess you appeared in front of me because the time was right. I need to make a decision now."

"What does your heart say about Yusuf?"

"I love him, Bahar. I haven't met a man who looks at me so beautifully before. I haven't tasted love. Actually, it was our shared sorrows that brought us closer. We drew different conclusions from them and determined our path. Our partnership there did not open our hearts. But Yusuf gave up before me. He offered his love so warmly and unconditionally that I considered this attitude I had never seen before as a weakness. There were moments when I hurt him because of it."

"Don't blame yourself for that. Don't we all look at life with our own codes? What matters now is that the eye of the heart has opened."

"It has, and because of that, I have started to see his heart's wounds, too. I know I can embrace him. I don't care what others will say or if they find him a good match for me. I don't remember ever loving someone so warmly, including my parents. It's worth a try, isn't it?"

I didn't answer that question. It was already clear that she didn't have such an expectation. After a short silence filled the air, I said, "Well, it's time to gather and hit the road," and I was glad to see Gamze jump up as if she had been waiting for it. In the meantime, we both laughed when she almost knocked over the table. How did we come? How were we leaving?

On the way back, I turned on the radio. We took turns predicting fortunes from the songs; we either got excited or got annoyed when we heard the lyrics. At least we sang the choruses out loud. It was already dark when we entered the city.

"Shall I drop you off at home?" I asked.

"No," she said, "I need to talk to Yusuf. It's time for me to look at him lovingly. He needs to see that I won't hold myself back any more, starting tonight. After all, he waited for a long time. I guess I'm having a hard time understanding it."

According to the directions, I took her to the door. I left the engine running and got out. I walked over to Gamze's side and hugged her tightly this time. "Be very happy! Develop where you're not happy. Return so you can continue," I said.

"What's that? It sounded like a farewell. You're not going anywhere, are you?" she asked anxiously.

"I feel that there's still a lot we can learn from each other. I felt like you were my sister on this trip. I will never let go…" I replied.

"Look, you said never! But let's admit it, it found its place here. Isn't that right, soul mate?" We both started laughing.

Yusuf had heard the noise of the old car's motor and came up to the entrance of the building. As he approached us, I moved to the driver's seat, waved from a distance, and left them behind. The last image I saw in the rearview mirror was them looking at each other so beautifully.

The veil that obstructs the sight is lifted. Once the veil is lifted, starting from personal experiences, all institutions and relationships that give meaning to personal existence are reevaluated. When the eyes open, the first thing seen is the complete opposite of what has been believed and trusted until then. This can be called the disillusioning effect. But even this, like a bewitched mind, is unreal.

— Entzauberung (disenchantment), Max Weber

Ruby Earrings

Was it a dream or not? Memories flooded into my mind, and I can't distinguish. Perhaps it's because I find myself between sleep and wakefulness. I gave my mother the ruby earrings. She was sitting on the couch, and I stood in front of her. I knelt before her. I held her hands with both of mine, opened her palms, then took out the earrings that I had put in my pocket before going there, using my right hand, and placed one in each palm, waiting. She didn't move. She simply lowered her eyes from my face and started to look at the earrings.

These earrings, too, came from her mother and were supposed to be passed on to the eldest daughter of the next generation when their owner passed away, according to the family tradition. No one remembered when this journey had started. Türkan, my grandmother, the one I was named after, had never seen her granddaughter, me. Nor my sister... Actually, even before having the chance to give the earrings to my mother, we lost my grandmother in a strange traffic accident. The earrings were still on her ears that day and were passed on to my mother along with her other personal belongings. My mother never took them off; that is, until the series of tomography and MRI scans she had to undergo one after another began. Each time she took them off and handed them to me, making sure to give me strict warnings. Not only because they caused worry for her and me, but also because there was a high risk of them getting lost amidst all the commotion, one day, she put them in the safe at home, and set the combination to my date of birth, thus implicitly sent the content on their way to the next owner. I can't recall how many years ago that was. Keeping a record of time, which sometimes sped by and sometimes dragged on, was not something I wanted to do.

Even long before I met Attila, I felt tired of having no expectations from life. Everything was going wrong; everything was a mess. You know how they say, "Whatever you touch turns to dust." Well, it was like being under such a curse. Though it might sound like an exaggeration, anyone living with me for just a month could feel what I meant down to their bones. I had long lost the desire to let anyone into my life, even for a few days; I'm saying this metaphorically. I was living with these nightmares all by myself. My mother, engrossed in her social projects for a long time, and not having to lament in front of her witness, accepted it as a significant energy saver. I even took up a project for her out of nowhere. When the suggestion came from me, she would pause for a moment, consider, and then claim the idea as her own, surprised at how such a thought could have occurred to her. Since I disappeared immediately after, the starting point of this idea was easily forgotten, and it spread to other areas with applause from that group. That's when I could bury myself in my own frustrations and not be saddened or surprised by the hopelessness of my future.

Attila entered my life like a story; he came hidden in a story that was too beautiful to be true but carried the hope that it could be real. If we had met him anywhere and anytime, just like I did with all the beauty, I would have hidden him in my deepest pit. The possibility of my mother finding out would have terrified me. Who knows what accusations she might make, what criticisms she would come up with out of nowhere, and smother him with? Even if she didn't, the fear of it would lead me to subconsciously drive Attila away. There must be a strong reason for me to be alone for so long, right? On the other hand, I couldn't settle down my instinct to get my mother's approval without getting approval from her. This dilemma, I couldn't bear it, but there was no time left. I could only realize much later that I was pulled into a vortex that my mother was at the center of it.

It was a time when days passed as usual. With the increase of her headaches, my mother went to the doctor, and they diagnosed her with a brain tumor. Thus, my mother became the main protagonist of an unprecedented struggle. A determination without any need for words to shoulder it together bonded us tightly. Even when she had only suspected cancer, my mother decided to do whatever was necessary, and even more. She mobilized all her social networks for this purpose. At that stage, I was like a mannequin accompanying her on the go. In fact, my role went beyond the responsibilities of running errands. I was constantly working behind the scenes to make her tasks faster and easier. Soon, Attila joined in, and the workload was divided, allowing me to breathe a little. Running after everything all by myself turned out to be even more exhausting than I had realized. My mother's encounter with Attila during that time was the result of an interesting coincidence. Everything else happened naturally. Attila owed his rise from an extra to the best male actor award to the admiration of two women.

During a period when she was hospitalized for treatment, my mother needed blood transfusions. We spread the word among a wide circle of friends since having the rarest blood type suited my mother's character. Even though it wasn't necessary, my mother had wanted to see the blood donor. She would ask, and I would fulfill; granting her wish was always easier than dealing with the difficulties that came with refusing. When I hesitantly told my friend, who was the contact person, about the situation, she said it was the most natural demand, opening the way for a chain of events. I learned the name and phone number of the person who donated blood to my mother. I gathered my courage and wanted to call right away, so I could get this matter off my mind and continue with more complicated tasks. At that time, Attila, or Mr. Atilla as formal then, quickly understood the desire I tried to explain away as stomach pain and asked about the most suitable time to visit my mother, saying his workplace was close to the hospital. I agreed to set up a meeting, which I initially found absurd. However, the way people around me considered it so natural and even went into action made me feel that the problem was with me. So, I reluctantly arranged the meeting. Thus, the two of them met for the first time.

When they met in the hospital room, I wasn't with them. I was busy arranging for someone to stay as a companion. We didn't have many options; my mother didn't want a caretaker, and my sister was taking care of so many things for her children and husband that she couldn't easily step out of that routine. Not previously raising my own family to take responsibility for allowing me to be more available. My work and personal life didn't seem to provide enough priority.

On the night of the business dinner I had to attend, I had arranged for my sister to come, so I rushed to the hospital to have some time before she arrived. At the time, the patient's bed was moved a little away from the wall and turned toward the television hanging on the opposite wall, where a nice gentleman was sitting. My mother had propped up the back of her bed and was standing tall like a nobleman in her pajama set, the color of a fawn, with lace-trimmed cuffs, collar, and hems, thanks to two pillows placed behind her to support her back. They were so engrossed in their conversation that they didn't notice my arrival for a while.

Finally, I decided to make a slight noise. I was content with just a little cough, as I didn't want to disturb the delicacy that had become palpable in the air while observing their interactions. I had brought my mother her favorite tahini pastry, fresh out of the oven, its aroma and steam still rising, but it had no stimulating effect. The conversation was so profound. Just a few seconds before they noticed me, my mother must have caught the smell because her reaction was very swift. "Türkan, Attila has come to visit me. He not only shared his blood, but also offered his friendship. I can't express how happy I am!"

I was taken aback by the tone of her theatrical lines, but I didn't show it. Moreover, when Mr. Atilla said, "Oh, Mrs. Müjgan, the happiness belongs to me. Listening to your wisdom-filled stories about life and your genuine friendship are the most valuable gifts for me!" I was left speechless. Feeling so surplus bothered me. Unfortunately, there was no way I could express it. I looked around. On the small refrigerator, an electric teapot was ready to serve. I had placed the tea in three glass cups, and I had divided the tahini pastry into four equal pieces, saving one for my sister.

Offering these treats hospitably to my mother and her guests seemed to be the only option, hoping they would accept my presence in their pleasant conversation. My interest in Mr. Atilla (Attila Bey) and the gratitude I felt for his role in this situation started from there.

Although we were able to discharge my mother from the hospital, she needed to continue her medical treatment as an outpatient. We had committed to memory the cycle of events;

going to the hospital, waiting for our turn, burying ourselves in our books during the slow infusion of medication to avoid feeling that we were wasting time, hoping there would be no side effects of the medication when they told us we could leave, and being surprised at how quickly the new appointment for medication came.

After her discharge, I made arrangements to take my mother to her first outpatient session when I learned that she had made an appointment with Attila Bey. Phone numbers had been exchanged, and meetings had already taken place. I remember feeling a bit jealous inside. I wasn't pleased to be pushed out as the only one who had taken on the entire process. She was my mother, and I was her daughter; no matter how much we argued, fought, or reconciled, it was unacceptable for her to prefer someone else's company. Besides, where did that someone else find the right to this?

An old, sick, and both delicate and stubborn (this combination irritated me the most) woman who already had at least one devoted daughter taking care of her. How could anyone think they had the right to spend time with her, listen to her desires carefully, and think about what would comfort her, without even informing me, and take action for it? Now, as I think back, I'm glad I didn't react to them with those emotions.

After a few encounters, when the situation changed direction, I slowly began to notice some things. I, who had always prided myself on grasping everything that was happening, found myself wrapped in my denials, anger about the impending loss, bargaining with myself and life, and trapped in my pain. Due to my condition, I never thought that any support would be as beneficial for me as it would be for my mother. If I had chosen to observe rather than prevent what was happening, I wouldn't even be aware of this whole cluster of possibilities that I had pushed away with the back of my hand.

As I was immersed in the other tasks I had been postponing, thinking that I didn't have to take my mother to the hospital anyway, my cell phone rang. The moment I saw my mother's name on the screen, I answered with a childlike reaction, thinking to myself, *See, it doesn't work without me, does it?* Despite the cold shower effect of facing this expectation, I managed to speak calmly. *"Hello, Mom; is everything OK?"*

My mother whispered in response, *"Türkan, I invited Attila for dinner. Try to be home in an hour."*

My blood rushed to my brain. I tried to say that we had no food at home, but my mother hung up as she said, *"Can't we at least make some soup and serve it?"* I had no chance to object that there was no noteworthy soup to make. Since she wouldn't prepare anything, the task was left to me. I quickly made my way home.

At the same time, I called the deli where I usually shopped and placed an order for a kilogram of *mantı* (small-sized Turkish-type ravioli), a medium-sized terracotta bowl of yogurt, and a small glass jar of homemade tomato paste, my first option that came to mind. I told the person on the phone that I would be home in half an hour. After hanging up, I wondered if we had garlic at home. There was no place I could stop on my way, but I comforted myself, thinking that my mother, who liked to put garlic in her dishes, would surely have some stored away. Besides, maybe our guest wouldn't want garlic in his yogurt. I chuckled; then he might never come to eat with us again. Despite all this rush, both the preparation and the meal went by easily.

My mother opened the door with her key without knocking and entered the house. I listened carefully, trying to understand what was going on. Even though the sound of the extractor fan obstructed my hearing, I realized that two people were talking, but I couldn't fully grasp their conversation. I didn't feel like going to greet them. If they acted as if I weren't there, why couldn't I do the same?

Shortly after, my mother came to me alone, and her face lit up when she smelled the delicious meat pasty. "You're amazing; I didn't even think of this. Now, I'll host a dinner with my favorite dish!" she said while clapping her hands. Then she mentioned that she left our guest to rest in the living room and asked him to choose one of the music CDs from the cabinet.

I was about to say that I didn't like these accompli arrangements, but before I could, she continued, "While you prepare the buttery tomato sauce, I'll crush some garlic for the yogurt. You said the other day that meal goes best with garlic yogurt. What did you think of this dish? Bravo, well done." Then she got to work.

I had already set the dinner table in the living room. All that was left was to place the meal on the plates and cover it with yogurt, tomato sauce, and at last dried mint on the top. That was done quickly, too. When I entered the living room holding two plates, Attila saw me and rushed over to take the plates from me. "I'm bothering you; I didn't refuse your mother's offer when she insisted. You must know how hard it is to say no to her," he said, planting the seeds of a secret alliance. I settled for smiling.

I headed to the kitchen to fetch the water pitcher and the last plate, but my mother was already bringing them. We sat down at the table together, and I realized that it had been a long time since we had such a richly conversational, laughter-filled, memorable, and sincere meal with my mother. Throughout the meal, the faint melodies playing in the background made it feel like we were spending an evening in a seaside restaurant on a summer night. It wouldn't have surprised me if Attila and I left my mother there and took a stroll along the coast.

After this first dinner, my mother's plan gradually unfolded. She did everything she could to bond us. When I heard that Attila would take us to our hometown, I was at a loss for words. When my mother suggested a temporary fake engagement as an excuse to make it easier to explain to relatives, I was furious at how much she pushed the boundaries. But Attila said it wasn't such a bad idea.

Even now, looking back on those days, I can't figure out the secret of my constant opposition and how everything that seemed natural to others felt unnatural to me. Could it just be fate, as my mother always said? According to her, fate requires small touches.

That trip was very interesting. It was impossible not to be affected by Attila's thoughtfulness and the positive impression he left on everyone he met. There were even some cousins who pulled me aside and said, "Don't let this man go; do whatever you can to make it last. You won't find anyone better."

What started as a game was branching out into something more. On the other hand, if we didn't end this theatrical engagement with a breakup announcement soon, I could easily get carried away. Neither my mother nor Attila seemed uneasy. They were really into their roles. At one point, when I was alone with Attila, I told him that I regretted putting him in this situation. He replied very calmly, "This is how it should be now. Don't worry. We'll see what happens later." I was able to detect traces of him adopting the role he played in his response.

My mother was truly happy. I expected her to think that not leaving me alone would prevent her from giving up on life despite the pains she would endure. According to her, everything was in its place except for my future happiness. She was burning with the desire to reunite with my father, her only love and passion for years. Therefore, while the cancer diagnosis wouldn't shake her, its timing objected to my perpetual loneliness.

Although I understood the motivation that drove her into these games and designs, I couldn't understand Attila's ease in participating. My only small haven inside me was that, even though it was based on a lie, my mother could set aside her concerns about me one day, considering the possibility of it coming true. At first, I would warn her and remind her of the truth, but I stopped because this wasn't what she wanted to hear. Besides, we had reached the stage where the doctors said to do whatever she wanted, whatever would make her feel alive.

Upon returning from the holiday, my mother deteriorated rapidly. It was as if she had used up all her strength to delay her downhill decline until then, and now she began to experience health problems one after another. In about two weeks, it was discussed that she would soon become bedridden, and there was even the possibility of being admitted to the intensive care unit. She was not the type of person who would end up in the ICU.

While lamenting why all this had happened to such a strong woman, I suddenly had an epiphany. I felt that I needed to trust her. I started to see that I, too, was affected by what was happening. I became softer toward life, more accepting of what it brought, and more attached to those who accompanied me during this time. I felt the hardest core inside me melting and blending with the rest. For the first time, I was becoming whole with myself. How painful it was for my mother to have to leave for this to happen. Besides giving birth and raising children, mothers had a significant role in allowing them to be themselves.

The final touch on what life did belong to the mother.

Since my mother's passing was approaching, I could see the meaning of the past more clearly. How everything had been left unfinished when my father suddenly passed away. I thought my mother, who loved my father, her soul mate, more than any of us, would refuse to be left behind and somehow find a way to follow him. Maybe, that's why I choose not to get too attached to my mother. The best antidote to the pain of loss was to ensure that it ended up not being a loss. If my subconscious created it this way back then, I wouldn't be surprised. However, by doing so, I couldn't manage to bond with life. It's so interesting how all these things filled my soul after such a long time.

I stand in front of my mother. "I'm leaving these ruby earrings with you; I don't want them anymore," I say as I place the earrings in her palms. When she lowers her eyes from my face to the earrings, I become hopeful. She will wear the earrings for the last time, and these nightmares will end. She clasps her two hands together, trapping the ruby earrings between her palms, shaking them, shaking them, and I wonder what she's going to do. I don't want her to stop; if she stops, she will die.

While in horror, I suddenly realize that the earrings are now on my ears. At that moment, I woke up from yet another endless dream. As I emerge from the fog between sleep and wakefulness, I realize that my mother has actually died. Trying to figure out where I am, I see Attila sleeping next to me. Suddenly, everything comes back to me.

I actually think I'm happy that I've made enough progress to find peace. But as I think that, I notice that I'm not convinced. I start to panic. If I toss and turn in bed, I will wake up Attila again, and I don't have the right to upset him. So I get up.

My mind is fixated on the ruby earrings. I haven't taken them out of the safe since my mother's death; I haven't even opened the safe. The dream is so vivid that I have to see the earrings; I have to let whatever happens happen. When I opened the safe, I'm very surprised to find an envelope under the small wooden box. When I saw my mother's handwriting on the letter inside the envelope, I started crying like a child with sobs. When all my tears are gone, I try to read the writing left behind in my tear-stained eyes.

"My *Gülpembe,* that's what we used to call you when you were a little girl. Do you remember? Because when you smiled, roses bloomed... Your father and I loved you so much. I loved your smile the most, and I loved making you laugh even more... I played so many games to make your face and heart smile again. I don't know what would have happened if Attila hadn't appeared. I would have left everything behind. I would have been in a terrible state. Your grandmother couldn't know your father; that's always been a regret for me. To see that you didn't abandon yourself while choosing a spouse was important to me for this reason. At the end of my journey, you gave me happiness that also untied the knot concerning myself. Don't forget this. I'm leaving with peace. May you also be at peace? Live your time to the fullest. May there be no regrets or sorrow within you. I waited for you. I waited to see that you found yourself. Every second was worth it. It was worth not being late. Now, both of us are in love. Value what you have. Your father would have wanted it this way. Now I can go to meet him. Let these words be an earring for you."

My hand was trembling when I picked up the box with the ruby earrings this time. When the palpitations in my heart subsided, I opened the lid and took out the earrings. They seemed shinier than before, and I put them on for the first time. Could I have been relieved all of a sudden? It's possible.

Until I find the next owner, I won't give up my earrings.

The Secret in the Mansion

I saw a grand mansion at the end of the road, with a slight slope that I pass by every day, on the peak I reached while gazing at the trees. It was neglected, abandoned, a ruin… I hadn't intended to go inside. I thought I would just wander around its surroundings and observe it from the outside. But I couldn't settle for that. Was it the allure of solitude that drew me? Was it the courage that led me to its imposing door, wishing it to be closed, to push open that massive door, or was it the thirst for adventure?

    The door opened with my tender touch. Right at that moment, I sensed that a completely different world was unfolding before me. The wide corridor at the entrance seemed to stretch into the depths of an endless tunnel. I walked on. The initial brightness of the entrance quickly faded. The small source of light that I didn't leave by my side came to my aid, casting a delicate pathway of light ahead of me. First, I turned to the windows to summon the daylight inside the first room I entered. The entry of light into the room had been hindered by wooden shutters nailed to the window frames. I tried every single window. None of them would open. Meanwhile, my eyes adjusted to the darkness. I started examining the interior. I sensed that the ceilings were ornate, but I couldn't make out the details. The floors were made of wood and quite worn. They creaked as if in pain with every step. I wandered through the empty rooms step-by-step. At their corners, I would either find a hidden cabinet and try to identify its reliefs by caressing them, or stumble upon a fireplace and, beyond my light, play with sparks in the flames of bygone times, clearing a path through the ashes. I was in a magical passage between a dreamlike world and reality. It was as if every corner of the mansion exuded memories. I could swear I smelled the intense scent of laurel soap by its basins.

My strings were in the hands of enthusiasm. While wandering, I reached a staircase that led to the upper floor. I headed toward its steps with determined strides. It was made of marble. It had broad and high steps. The underside was completely flat, and no area resembled a joint. It seemed like a huge marble piece had been carved into a staircase. For the first time since the beginning, I stepped on the ground with confidence; no creaking, no shaking. After the staircase, there was again the uncertainty of wooden floorboards. Nonetheless, I started to explore the upper floor. At the ceiling part that matched the staircase gap, there was an area with leftover space in the incredible shades of green mosaics. When I regained the daylight, my mood increased by another level. When I discovered that there were other openings to the sky, my excitement grew even more. Although the mansion extended in all directions, it was enclosed by terraces that were made independent of each other. I was no longer afraid of the loneliness of the mansion. It was as if I wasn't alone already. Just when I thought my excitement was calming down, my palpitations were subsiding, I found a new excitement waiting for me on the large terrace.

A young girl was sitting with her face turned to the view outside. Her hair was black as night, swaying in the breeze as it sang. From the very first moment, it pulled me into its strings and offered unheard melodies. When I managed to free myself from the pull of her hair and focused on her details, I saw the rose in front of her. Childlike joy filled my heart and my face. This person was sitting in front of a single rose without getting bored, without losing interest, observing it. I remembered the fox of Little Prince. "What makes your rose so important is the time you have spent on it!" he used to say. I used to see birds of luck around me. Moreover, this wasn't the first time. Whenever I felt close to someone, they would appear.

I approached the young girl gently from behind. Now, I wanted to know her through realities rather than intuitions. I needed to listen to what she would tell me in her own words, looking into her eyes. "Even though I had to go through all its leaves, even though its thorns pierced my skin, I tried to get to know the rose. At first, I perceived the calls that brought me to it. I waited without touching and got used to being near it. The pain of the first thorn made the presence of the rose certain. I became afraid to touch it again. Eventually, I succumbed to my inner desire. I reached the softness of its petals. My fingers slipped. With this feeling, I lost myself. The thorns always appeared in unexpected moments, hurting me. When I got used to them and accepted this pain, I learned to avoid the thorns," the young girl explained. She couldn't see. With her eyes fixed on a point, she expressed her passion for the rose. I started to understand how inadequate images were at that moment. And there were the experiences in the heart. However, we were resisting, not using the path that extended from our eyes to our hearts. There was a curtain between the two of them that we didn't want to lift.

She seemed to be happy because she couldn't see my face. "It's better this way," she said and added, "I can give you any appearance I want. If my heart doesn't approve of your existence, you can't be more than a voice. But if I embrace you and love you, there will be a representative of color in me. And of course, there's the image I've assigned to you, the one I've engraved in my memory with my fingertips."

It felt strange for her to talk about colors. She couldn't see them, and there was no way for her to understand through touch. If I told her that the red rose in front of her was yellow, she had to believe it. I was about to ask for an explanation when she interrupted.

"Don't stop. Say you don't believe me. I also don't believe in your colors. You name them on the first encounter; pink carnation, hazel eyes... How can you know? You haven't known them for long enough for them to reveal their colors. My colors emerge as I live. They can transform into each other. Like life, they are not static either. Sometimes, it's a carnival of colors that I experience." She continued the conversation with a genuine explanation. "When I learned that I would never see again, sorrow filled me. I had no doubt that I would be plunged into complete darkness. I understood that I had to hold on to avoid being lost. With the sensitivity of a baby just beginning to know life, with the curiosity of a baby, I had to reach out to everything, just as much as a baby would do. I had to learn to recognize the traces it left on my hands. Only the colors, I thought, I would miss. The solution was within me again. I mixed its memories with my emotions. My own colors emerged. I quickly embraced them; they were not strangers. Now, every time I fill with hope, I live in white; when I cling to hope, when I dream of beginnings, when I expect beauty, I experience the white."

I had been drawn into an unfamiliar game. I was taking emotions in one hand and colors in the other. Mixing and opening them, and each time, I was surprised. The eyes of my beloved, which I have no doubt were brown, were looking at me in shades of pink from my palm. It was the dreams I saw every time I dived into these eyes that gave this color. The mountains in front of me were purple; because they evoked a sense of sadness being tied up. Journeys were red; wanting to leave passionately, adventures were always red... Blue defined not being able to stay still, playing with wild waves... Black was fear; whatever the reason... Yellow held longing, longing for whatever it might be.

"Are you alone?" a voice said.

I turned around. A man. He and I were alone on the terrace. "There was a girl and a rose..."

My voice was trembling. With this stranger, it felt as if a breeze hit my face. Both of us looked around. We couldn't see anyone on the terrace. I didn't try to search for the girl. And telling this man about someone's existence would be in vain. He was doing his duty, trying to bring back the old solitude to the mansion by driving away an unauthorized intruder. Suddenly, I realized that it was late. Taking my colors and the red rose left on the terrace with me, I rushed away from the mansion.

The night was twilight. The moon was blue. Me? Certainly, whiter than white...

Silent Farewell

Mother, you should come tonight. I've been waiting for this meeting for a whole year, but you never came. Tonight, or never... It's black and white. I no longer have the strength for grays. Especially tonight. I need to see you, hear you; more than ever before. I am asking for a night that will connect all the times before tomorrow morning. I need it as much as I need air... Come, don't let me drown. Meet me tonight; tell, understand, so I can breathe again.

What a great fortune it has been, to reach you whenever I wanted... To be able to openly discuss every contradiction, design, and action I've taken, everything I've built or crumbled with you, was such a special privilege. How I long for the healing power of your words, the strength I felt when you whispered that we could solve a problem together by embracing it tightly, believing that nothing bad could reach me when you were by my side. If I say that the moments of happiness I occasionally feel, though not comparable to the previous ones, have no meaning unless I share them with you, would you, the person I want to make proud, be mad at me? You would, I know. You can't stand seeing me weak, hopeless, aimless like this. So come and shake me; just like you used to do, shake me to bring me back to myself. Renew my self-confidence, make me believe that everything will be beautiful again; once more...

I haven't called for you in a year. I held back because I knew that if I did it when I really needed to, I would achieve a result. I restrained myself back. Now what I want to ask you, to be able to see you, has taken on a different meaning. Maybe I'm exaggerating again, and I can't realize this on my own. If you were here, you could turn my perception in a direction that would comfort me. You could make me see that it's really nothing more than a simple ceremony. I know that's all it means to you. We've never talked about it. Even though I knew you had such an idea in your mind, I think I chose not to think about it. Whatever was necessary would be done when the time came. I didn't realize how much I secretly wished that time never came. Now, I don't even know if I'm ready for it.

My mother hasn't been with me for a year. What I said might be true in a physical sense, but I live with her every moment. I keep her alive within me. I console myself this way. On the other hand, in recent months, I've started to realize that without her touch, this perspective becomes an illusion. Yes, for a year, I've been moving forward with the answer to the question, "How would my mother do this?" at every stage.

Although I usually trust my choices without hesitation, sometimes the thought that my mother would do it better overshadows my actions at that moment. After observing her so closely for twenty years, emulating her, imitating her, and internalizing her, I think I'm certain, but I'm worried that I'll be tested with more special moments of decision-making after this time, and making judgments without experiencing similar situations will be difficult, even misleading.

I'm beginning to see that it's not enough to walk in the footsteps of such a strong and productive woman, a guide who has touched the lives of everyone, adult and child, who crossed her path. Yes, I can sense that my small steps won't be enough.

However, I'm avoiding admitting this to myself. To admit to myself that I can't do it now without her touch is a terrifying idea. Yes, for a year, I've been advancing at every stage by asking myself, *"How would my mother do this?"* But without her, this perspective becomes an illusion.

"I knew you would come, Mom. You would never deny me this chance."

"I might not have been able to come. Despite wanting to very much, there might not have been a way."

"I'm glad you found a way, Mom, and that you did it again."

"I'm happy too. You know, I never wanted to disappoint you."

"How could you ever disappoint me? Not just me, you can't do it for anyone who enters your life. If you knew what was said behind you, what stories were told... I didn't realize the true meaning of many things you did while you were with me. I could see them better when they were recounted by those influenced by your actions, your directions, your words."

"I'm glad I found time for these things. And I'm glad to see you and your brother grow up. I may have accomplished many projects, but you should know that you were my most precious projects. What I am most proud of is my children I left behind."

"You always made us feel how much of a source of pride we were for you. That felt good. That's why there are moments when I flounder in your absence. Sometimes, I struggle because I can't draw support from your presence, not just from my memories."

"Do you know why I trust you unconditionally?"

"Is that true?"

"Of course, because all this time, I watched your wings dry out with great excitement. You can trust them. Think about it this

way, if you weren't ready, your wings wouldn't have allowed you to fly."

"It's good to hear that. You can be sure I'll repeat it to myself many times."

"Your reason for wanting me to come here wasn't to discuss these things, was it?"

"You're right. I don't know how to say it. I guess this time too, I'm afraid of disappointing you. On the other hand, I feel like I'm not ready to leave you yet."

"Why did you think we were going to part?"

"What remains of you, we'll scatter it to the wind and the sea tomorrow. We agreed to do this as a family on the first anniversary. I know this is what you wanted. Of course, I respect it. Still, I fear that if you disperse in nature, I will also disperse in life."

"My presence in our home this past year, being a safe haven for you, that was important. Think of it as a transitional phase. But now the time has come to set you free, to leave you to life. You've won several small victories during this time, proving that you can cope with life."

"It was comforting to know that I would find you there when I arrived home."

"Think of it this way, now I'll be everywhere."

"So, can I continue to feel you whenever I need to?"

"I don't need to be in one place or scattered around the world for that; I'll be in your thoughts; in every awareness I've created within you. Some of the things I've given you will lose their impact and disappear over time. I wanted your roots to be strong; because you will always come back to me, my daughter."

"Mother, I think I'm starting to understand you."

"I'm sure of it. Now I have to go. Good morning."

I immediately ran to my father. I knew I would find him in the garden. I had no doubt he was watching the sunrise over the sea. His sleep had been untimely; untimely and fragmented. While I had gotten used to finding him in unexpected places, at that moment I realized that a different routine had begun to emerge. As soon as I opened the garden gate, a warm scent of jasmine hit me. My joy was so great that it might have been audible to my father. When he turned around and saw me, a warm smile spread across his face. I ran and hugged him.

"Dad, I dreamed of my mother. She was so beautiful that she was dazzling. And she was so alive."

"I know, my dear."

"I talked about all the questions in my head with her. I wanted to say goodbye. This was an unstoppable wish. Moreover, it had to happen before this morning. I was so afraid that she wouldn't come, Dad."

"I want to show you something."

"What is it? Where is it? Can I see it right now?"

"Under the jasmine tree in the garden. Come, let's go. Your mother wants to say goodbye with that jasmine she planted for all her flowers."

"This is what I would certainly want to see. Look, our dog is waiting there too."

My father and I went over to the jasmine tree. There, I saw a square-shaped box made of marble. On the cover that covered it, my mother's name and birthdate were written. I couldn't make sense of it. For a while, I couldn't realize how long it lasted. I silently stared at that name. Then, with questioning eyes, I looked at my father. When he decided to break his silence, he began to tell the story. My mother always made her decisions and executed her plans as they were. Her decisions were so well-thought-out that once they were put into action, no changes were needed. She left no room for possibilities, never relying on conditional plans like 'If this happens, we'll do that; if that doesn't happen, we'll do this.' Furthermore, I've never witnessed her calculations going awry. This time, she had decided that her body would be cremated, and then the ashes would remain in a box at our home for a year, and on the first anniversary, they would be scattered into the wind and the sea right in the middle of the scene that had captivated her. She saw this view, and we immediately bought the land to build our summerhouse, where we shared beautiful memories afterward. That was her decision. I had checked the small wooden box one last time before falling asleep last night.

But now my father was telling me that my mother's ashes were in this marble box. According to his account, my mother had prepared one more option that she had only told my father about. The alternative to scattering the ashes was to be left securely in a marble box and then placed in the sea. Since my mother couldn't decide which one she wanted, she told my father to make the preparations and wait. What he had told me up to that point had surprised me greatly. As I tried to understand, I couldn't bring the question I really needed to ask to my mind. Suddenly, it spilled out of my mouth, "So why did the marble box emerge now?"

"Last night, I knew she would come to my dreams. She wouldn't leave me in doubt. According to her wish, I had prepared everything for our ceremony in the morning. There was only one detail that remained uncertain. Even though I don't need dreams to talk to her, this time I wanted us to stand face to face as close to reality as possible, to talk to each other while looking at each other, and finally, to find out her decision. Just as I had imagined, it happened. We were in the park where we used to take walks together in my dream. It was the park she loved to play in during her childhood and the first place she took me to introduce me to her past. We were on the narrow paths she liked to walk, with me by her side. These paths were so narrow that in her final days, she would walk with her arm around mine, and I thought I could carry her like this forever. We stood facing each other under the tree where I first kissed her, and we looked at each other. We talked about many things. When I woke up, even though they weren't in my mind, a peaceful feeling lingered within me. And then, I felt that she wanted to be placed in the marble box and dropped into the sea… I was secretly very glad about this. I would know where to go. I would get on the boat and come to her side. I would leave a seashell on her bedside table, which I would take out of my pocket."

For the last year, I took on a responsibility that my mother had without telling anyone. She never missed an opportunity to gather the whole family together, ensuring that all these different lives converged and united around big and crowded tables. Today is such a time. I had insisted on finishing the preparations and going out to sea. When we returned, seeing all my mother's loved ones gathered around a table would be the antidote to the possible feeling of loneliness for all of us. My guess was correct.

Throughout the entire meal, a strong and warm scent of jasmine touched each of us.